Cry in a Long Night
and Four Stories

written by **Jabra Ibrahim Jabra**

translated by **William Tamplin**

 **DARF PUBLISHERS**

Darf Publishers, 2022
277 West End Lane
West Hampstead
London, NW6 1QS

Cry in a Long Night and Four Other Stories by Jabra Ibrahim Jabra

Originally published as *Surakh fi layl tawil* by Matba'at al-'Ani, Baghdad, 1955.

The four stories were published as *Araq, al-Mughannun fi al-zilal, al-Gharamafun, and al-Shijar* in the collection *Arak and Other Stories* (originally published as *Araq wa-qisas ukhra in Beirut by al-Mu'assasah al-ahliyyah li-l-tiba'ah wa-l-nashr* in 1956). Tawfiq Sayigh's study *Across the Wasteland* was published as the introduction to the same volume.

English translation by William Tamplin
Copyright © William Tamplin
All rights reserved

Cover designed by Luke Pajak

ISBN Paperback: 9781850773436
ISBN eBook: 9781850773443

Acknowledgements

For their support and encouragement throughout my translation of this novel, I thank Marc Shell, Bill Granara, Salim Tamari, Tania Nasir, Sadeer Jabra, Ozzy Gunduz, Aladdin Abukhait, Caroline Kahlenberg, John Cleaver, Max Nova, Tom Schuhmann, Roger Allen, Ghassan Fergiani, Sherif Dhaimish, Luke Pajak, Charlie Forrest, and Clare Richards.

Acknowledgements

Foreword
by Roger Allen

When Adnan Haydar and I decided in the late 1970s, as I now recall, to translate into English Jabra Ibrahim Jabra's novel, *al-Safīna* (1970), we were both already abundantly aware of the fact that the author was himself a superb and renowned translator of the most challenging of English literary works into Arabic – Shakespeare's tragedies and sonnets, for example, and, equally complex in a different way, William Faulkner's *The Sound and the Fury*. Soon after we started the translation project, Jabra happened to be paying a visit to New York. We both went up to see him at the Waldorf Astoria Hotel. During discussions of translation, Jabra was eager to point out to us that, while he was comfortable translating English works into Arabic, the reverse was not the case. He had set out once to translate his poem, *Urkudī, urkudī, yā muhratī*, into English, but, as the poet-creator of the original, he had found the translation process not only difficult but, in the end, unsatisfactory (his version was reprinted as 'Run, run, my lovely mare' in the literary journal *Edebiyat* 1 no. 2 [1976]: 146-7).

We set to work on the translation (*The Ship*, 1985), dividing the two principal narrators between us (I can reveal that I was the first English-language translator of Wadīʿ ʿAssāf), then sending the initial results to the other, before sending them to Jabra himself for his comments. Being pre-Internet, what we sent was on paper, and the pages that came back were covered in suggestions – a clear reflection of Jabra's wonderful expertise in literary English style. That said, however, he was insistent that this was to be a translation and we were the translators. In a typical gesture, he even suggested that our English version of his novel would convey his intentions better than his Arabic original, in that our two different roles as first translators could capture the separate voices of his two narrators, Wadīʿ and ʿIṣām, more effectively than he had been able to do as the sole author of the novel. And, when Jabra sent each of us a copy of his later novel, *al-Baḥth ʿan Walīd Masʿūd* (1978), we adopted the same translation strategy, this time dividing the twelve narrative voices between us, while working together on the immensely complex first chapter, consisting of a punctuation-less transcript of a tape-recording (*In Search of Walid Masoud*, 2000).

During my visit to Baghdad in 1988 to participate in the
Marbid Poetry Festival, it was my incredible good fortune
to encounter Jabra in person again. During one evening
session of the festival conference, in which we were
listening to endless poetic accolades to Saddam Hussein,
Jabra inquired politely as to whether I was interested in
listening to any more of this kind of poetry or would
prefer instead to go to his house for supper. The choice
was simple, and I was privileged to visit his lovely home in
the Al-Mansur district of the city. The room where we sat
was filled with paintings, floor-to-ceiling shelves of books
(along with the necessary ladder to retrieve the volumes on
the highest level), and…a large collection of long-playing
records devoted to classical music. It was on this occasion
that Jabra became aware of my secondary profession as a
church musician, specifically as organist and choirmaster
of my university's Episcopal parish. He told me that he had
a particular liking for choral music from the earlier periods
of the classical tradition – the great Italians, Monteverdi
and Palestrina, for example, for Bach, of course, and, to
my surprise, for Henry Purcell. That particular evening
was to mark the beginning of what, for me, was a precious
musically-based relationship with its accompanying series
of memories. Throughout the years of conflict in Iraq,
I would send Jabra in Baghdad tape-recordings of his
favorite kind of music, some of them involving myself
on the organ and the choir that I directed. How poignant

was it, therefore, when he made a point of informing me that one of the characters in *al-Baḥth ʿan Walīd Masʿūd* is described as listening to the Purcell Suite that I had recently sent him. Later, those treasured memories of my visit to Jabra's home and our epistolary exchanges on music and other matters were to be reflected in the publication of a selection of his letters to me, entitled 'My dear Roger' (*Jusoor* Vols. 9/10 [1997/8]: 360-93). And how devastating was it to receive a phone-call from the late Anthony Shadid of the *New York Times* in 2010, informing me that Jabra's home had been blown up by a bomb, the perpetrators apparently mistaking his house for the Egyptian Embassy next door.

This translation introduces its readers to what was and is Jabra's first novel in Arabic (1955), although it seems to have had a pre-history of its own. According to Jabra himself, it was originally written in English in the 1940s, then rendered by him into Arabic while he was a research fellow at Harvard University in the 1950s. A copy of the English version, entitled *Passage in the Silent Night*, was destroyed, along with many other artistic and literary treasures, in the bombing of his house to which I referred above.

The narrative technique of this novel reflects its early placement in Jabra's development as a novelist. However, while it may not, as yet, resort to the complex multi-narrator formats of some of his later works, it certainly shows a ready awareness of other features of the developing novelistic tradition, with their various modes of penetration into the psychological make-up of character and invocations of memory – with their concomitant musings about human nature. It is set in an unnamed city, one that certainly bears a strong resemblance to Jerusalem (with its 'Old City'), during the highly unstable and tense period following World War II and immediately preceding the transformative year 1948 – the United Nations' 1947 declaration leading to the establishment of Israel as a state, the subsequent conflict, and the Palestinian '*nakba*' (catastrophe). And yet, as the novel's principal character and first-person narrator, Amīn Sammā', roams the city (which he describes as 'hell') and talks to acquaintances and friends, he seems strangely preoccupied by his own personal problems, not the least of which are his relationships with two women: one his wife, who has suddenly left him without warning, the other the daughter of a prominent family about which he is supposed to be writing a biography. Among other things, the narrator himself is writing a novel, but it is his wife's unexplained departure that has led him to 'wander in the lethal labyrinths of the past.' Critical commentary on Jabra's novel seems united in its observation that, as a reflection of his familiarity with Western creative fictional invocations of the mythic dimension (not least inspired by his translation during the same period of sections from James Frazier's famous, *The Golden Bough*), he has a broader cultural purpose in mind than a more traditionally realistic portrayal of current social and political tensions.

After reading the four stories from Jabra's collection, '*Araq* (1956), included in this volume, I have come to the conclusion, as someone who has devoted a good deal of attention to the analysis and translation of the modern Arabic short story genre, that Jabra's contributions belong in a category of their own. Their elaborate descriptions, their copious conversations, and, above all, their narrative style, suggest that they might best be construed as a set of scenarios, ideas for potentially longer narratives that were initial products of Jabra's fertile imagination but were not to be elaborated at novelistic length, being expressed instead in their current form. And it is with those narrative features in mind that these stories can take their place as ideal adjuncts to this published translation of Jabra's very first venture into novelistic composition.

In conclusion, I return to the musical theme. Jabra's last letter to me before his death in 1994 is a lengthy and detailed expression of his great delight in attending a concert in Amman in 1991, at which a song-cycle based on his poetry was performed. The singer was the soprano, Tania Nasir, who, along with her husband, Hanna, president of Birzeit University, was a longtime advocate for Palestinian causes and a friend of Jabra. During the intervals between songs, the camera recording the performance turns to show the open-air scene and the audience, with Jabra himself, prominently seated in the front row, clearly relishing this musical interpretation of his poetry. Music and poetry, united in song, and sung by a friend. What a perfect combination for a writer so devoted to art and its many and varied modes of expression!

Roger Allen
July 2020

Translator's Preface
by William Tamplin

Cry in a Long Night was a strange book to translate into English. Not least of all because *Cry in a Long Night* was originally written *in* English. The author, Jabra Ibrahim Jabra (1919-1994), claimed to have written this novel in English in Jerusalem in the summer of 1946. Jerusalem then was an apocalyptic city fraught with random explosions and terrorist violence as the British Mandate over Palestine slowly expired and the two local communities, Jewish Israeli and Palestinian Arab, which had crystallized during the Mandate years, prepared for war. In January 1948, in the midst of civil war, Jabra fled to Baghdad, taking his English novel with him.

Jabra originally entitled the work *Passage in the Silent Night*, and it was in fact his second English-language novel. He wrote his first, unpublished novel, *Echo and the Pool*, shortly after returning to Jerusalem, having spent four years in the UK studying English literature on a British Council scholarship. *Passage in the Silent Night* became *Cry in a Long Night* in the years 1952-1954, when Jabra translated it from English to Arabic and made certain emendations. During those years, he was living not in Baghdad but in a basement apartment at 60 Ellery Street in Cambridge, Massachusetts, where he was studying literary criticism at Harvard University on a Rockefeller Fellowship arranged personally by John Marshall, head of the Rockefeller Foundation's Humanities division. Just as he had studied at Cambridge with luminaries of literary criticism, F. R. Leavis and I. A. Richards, at Harvard, Jabra studied with Archibald MacLeish. Throughout his life, Jabra had one foot firmly in Anglophonia and another in his native Arab world. So on some level it makes perfect sense that Jabra's English novel came into being in a sweltering Jerusalem summer, while the English novel was transformed into an Arabic one in hoary old New England.

What happened to the original English version? And how does my translation compare to Jabra's original? We may never know. Jabra's son Sadeer, who grew up in Baghdad and now lives in Auckland, wrote to me that he supposed that the original was lost in the explosion that destroyed the Jabra family home in Baghdad on Easter Sunday 2010: a suicide bomber targeted the Egyptian embassy down the road, and the explosion destroyed most of the street, killing dozens of civilians, wounding hundreds of others, and destroying the library of one of the twentieth century's greatest Arabic writers. As much as I would have loved to see the original text of *Passage in the Silent Night*, I do wonder whether finding it would have affected my translation.

This novel is important in the context of Jabra's oeuvre because it lays the foundations for his later fictional output. It's told in the first person by the main character and narrator, 28-year-old Amin Samaa, an Arab Christian born and raised in the allegorical 'village', who moves with his family to the allegorical 'city' after his father dies. Amin, whose first name means 'faithful and true', grows up poor and, through study, enters the ranks of the new bourgeoisie, whom he never misses a chance to pillory – he watches them, listens to them, and records their ways with the sensitivity of a seismograph. Amin's surname *Sammāʿ* is an intensive form of the root that has to do with listening; he is an attentive listener. Amin works as a novelist in the morning and a journalist during the day. He has three novels to his name, which have brought fame, status and money to the social-climbing *arriviste* from the country. By night, Amin is helping an aristocratic heiress, Inayat Yasser, write a 150,000-word history of her family alongside the history of the city, covering the preceding 300 years. This project involves poring over family letters, papers and diaries in Ottoman Turkish and in Arabic in the Yasser family palace's basement for a few hours every night. Inayat, along with her sister Roxane, is unmarried and extremely wealthy.

The book takes place over the course of one long night as Amin traverses his native city, walking from his home on one side of it to the Yasser family palace on the other. One can imagine a similar walk for Jabra, who lived in West Jerusalem (Katamon) in his 20s and was a frequent guest of the (Yasser-like) Antonius family, who lived in the palace of the exiled Palestinian Grand Mufti al-Hajj Muhammad Amin al-Husayni, in Shaykh Jarrah in the eastern part of the city. The most direct route from Katamon to Shaykh Jarrah takes you through Zion Square, the heart of Jerusalem then and now, and perhaps the inspiration for the 'heart of the city' in *Cry in a Long Night*. One can imagine Jabra dreaming up this novel on his long walk home after an evening at the Antonius home. While Amin walks, his mind finds its way back to his relationship with his estranged wife Sumaya, his village childhood, his relationship with his father, and his poor upbringing.

Jabra wrote that the city he portrays in *Cry in a Long Night* was supposed to be an allegorical pan-Arab city. Yet there's ample evidence that Jabra drew heavily on his experience of pre-1948 Jerusalem for this novel. The action of the novel is located in a hilly city with a walled Old City; Amin recalls the idyllic village that was his childhood home located just twenty kilometers away (for Jabra, Bethlehem); a policeman checks the IDs of passersby (British-Mandate Jerusalem was divided); the two aristocratic heiresses and spinster sisters of the Yasser family call to mind Katy Antonius, the Jerusalem socialite and widow of the Arab nationalist (and then-late) George Antonius (1891-1942), whose *soirées* Jabra attended in pre-1948 Jerusalem; Amin works as a journalist (Jabra wrote articles for local newspapers after his return to Jerusalem in 1943); the Yasser sisters' illustrious ancestor and founder of their line, 'Tajeddine,' conquered the city while he was a lieutenant of Saladin's (by now, the city must be Jerusalem); and the novel features a double explosion (in the summer of 1946, a double explosion brought down King David Hotel, located two kilometers up the road from Jabra's home in Katamon). Despite the decidedly Jerusalemite air, readers of Jabra's autobiographies might also notice certain elements of the novel's plot and characters that must have been drawn from his post-1948 life in Baghdad, and thus well after he claimed this novel was first written. Some of those elements are: his fraught relationship with his future in-laws after he began seeing his future wife Lami'a (Jabra had to skip town for almost two years for Baghdad society to absorb the scandal of a Christian man marrying a Muslim woman); and the *existentialist conversations* that were a fixture of Baghdad cafe life in the 1950s (Jabra elaborates on them in *Princesses' Street*). Amin's despair at Sumaya's disappearance could have been a reflection of Jabra's frustration that his new wife Lami'a (m. 1952) was not able to join him for much of the time that he spent at Harvard, when he translated this novel. Jabra portrays his courtship with Lami'a within the Baghdad milieu in great detail in his autobiography, *Princesses' Street* (1994), and in his novel, *Hunters in a Narrow Street* (1959).

My interest in where Jabra pulled different elements of the novel's plot and characters from his own life stems directly from Jabra's own anxiety about the matter. Throughout the years, he insisted that although *Cry* was published in Baghdad in 1955, it had been written nine years earlier, in 1946, when he was a 26-year-old English teacher living with his family in Jerusalem. Later editions of the novel even erroneously list the date of the novel's first publication as 1946. Setting the book's publication date that far back would have allowed Jabra to claim a precocity that was his to claim anyway. *Cry in a Long Night* was ahead of its time when it eventually came out in 1955, so it goes without saying that the novel would have been a novelty nine years earlier.

Cry was the one of the first Arabic novels – if not the first – to employ stream of consciousness, flashback and interior monologue. Perhaps unsurprisingly, Jabra cites James Joyce, Aldous Huxley, D. H. Lawrence and Virginia Woolf as having been his greatest influences when he began writing fiction in the 1940s. Apart from his day job teaching English at a secondary school in Jerusalem, Jabra had just spent four continuous years in England during World War II immersed in British literature, studying all that English tripos at Cambridge required in those days. He was very close with his Censor, William Sutherland Thatcher, and his tutor, Helena Mennie Shire. He dated, attended plays, went by the name 'Gabriel,' hiked in the Lake District, fell in love with Renaissance choral music, and was affiliated with Fitzwilliam House, which, among a deserted wartime campus, had been converted into a military hospital. Fortunately for Jabra, Cambridge was spared all but a few bombing raids from the Luftwaffe; the town was eerily quiet. Take that young Palestinian man, put him back in his childhood home, much changed since he had last seen it in 1939, and let him write a novel. That is how the world got *Cry in a Long Night*. Indeed, the novel's influences are practically laid out in the annual report of the Jerusalem YMCA for 1945: Jabra was the founder of the YMCA's 'Arts Club,' which hosted lectures and poetry readings and put on artistic exhibitions, and the Club's 1944 schedule features events on Dante, Shelley and Watteau, whose poetry and paintings – for example, Shelley's 'Ozymandias' and Watteau's *The Embarkation for Cythera* – inspired Jabra's imagery in this novel. Jabra also draws on his childhood home in Jerusalem's (since demolished) neighborhood of Jorat al-'Innab (Jujube Hollow) in the stories 'The Fight' and 'The Gramophone' and Bethlehem in 'Singers in the Shadows.'

I should also mention this novel's title and the confusion

it has caused students and scholars of Arabic literature. The novel's title has been rendered by scholars variously as *Screams in a Long Night*, *A Scream in a Long Night*, *Screaming in the Long Night*, etc. Apart from the fact that Jabra himself rendered this novel's title as *Cry in a Long Night* in a 1981 interview, 'screams' does not capture it. The 'cry' of the title, *Surakh fi layl tawil*, is an Arabic verbal noun from the root *s-r-kh*, which has to do with screaming, crying out, calling out, yelling, bellowing. So 'crying out' might be the most literal, but not the most artful, rendering. The 'cry' of the title is a *cry of existential despair*, the howl of an outcast prophet. It is not a bout of weeping; it is not a scream of anger or outrage or fear. It contains the same verbal root as the mantic 'Voice *crying out* in the wilderness, Prepare a way for the Lord!' (Hebrew: *qol qore' ba-midbar*; Arabic: *sawt sarikh fi al-barriyyah*) from the Arabic translation of Isaiah. Jabra was raised a Syriac Orthodox Christian in Bethlehem, the birthplace of Christ. He would have been familiar with the text of the Old Testament from his childhood days at the local Syriac school, newly established by the refugee community. Jabra was also culturally literate and up-to-date with modern English literature: T. S. Eliot had drawn from Isaiah in his poem 'The Waste Land,' which Jabra loved and studied; his friend Tawfiq Sayigh also translated Eliot's poem. The 'cry' from the title, then, is from the Arabic *s-r-kh*, related through Isaiah to the Hebrew *q-r-'*, which is related to the Arabic *q-r-'*. And the Arabic *q-r-'* was the root of the *first word* of the *first surah* that God revealed to Muhammad through the angel Gabriel (Jabra means 'Gabriel') in 622 CE: 'Cry out! *(iqra'!)* In the name of your Lord who has created…' So, Jabra's 'cry' bridges the gap from divine revelation to the modern Palestinian novel; from one first to another. As the Israeli critic Matityahu Peled has written, Jabra's debut novel was a prophecy of the 'doom' about to befall the Palestinian people in 1948: around 700,000 Palestinians, the vast majority of whom were civilian non-combatants, would be expelled from their homes, and more than 400 Palestinian villages would be systematically destroyed by (or repopulated with) the Jewish Israeli conquerors. In foreseeing the Palestinian disaster of 1947-48, Jabra was a kind of prophet, what the Syrian critic Faysal Darraj has called a 'prophet-intellectual.' And indeed, in *Princesses' Street*, Jabra associates himself with John the Baptist, who called himself that 'voice crying out in the wilderness' in the Gospel of John. Jabra may have seen himself as later critics saw him: as a prophetic voice, like the Angel Gabriel or John the Baptist, whose leadership in the field of artistic and cultural modernization would usher in the redemption of Palestine.

Jabra Ibrahim Jabra was a complicated man who kept many secrets from his public. He created a convincing persona as a pioneering modernist in Arabic literature and a consummate autobiographer over nearly sixty years of literary production. Yet throughout his life, Jabra lied about his birthplace and family history, allowing friends, colleagues, and scholars to believe that because he was raised in Bethlehem, he must also have been born there. Jabra was actually born in the city of Adana, now located in Turkey, to a family of genocide survivors from Tur Abdin, a mountainous region in southeastern Anatolia considered the heartland of Syriac Christianity. When Jabra was born in Adana on 28 August 1919, the city was part of the short-lived Mandate of Cilicia, established by the French after World War I to protect local Christians, many of whom were war refugees (and to grab the fertile land around the Seyhan River). However, the French retreated before Ataturk's army, which reconquered the city and slaughtered many of the Christians who had not fled. Over the preceding thirty years, and beginning in around 1895, the Ottoman leadership and military, along with Kurdish irregulars, had systematically slaughtered four million Christians (Assyrians, Greeks, and Armenians) living in Anatolia in order to ethnically cleanse Anatolia of non-Muslims. Jabra's mother's first husband, Dawood, and her twin brother, Yusuf, had both been slaughtered by a Muslim mob in Adana in 1909. So it is fortunate that Jabra's family escaped to Bethlehem when they did, in the early 1920s. Why Jabra never mentioned his traumatic family history is a mystery. Perhaps it was too much for him to countenance. Perhaps it distracted from both his profound sense of Palestinian identity and his lifelong project to modernize the Arab world culturally and artistically as a means of advancing Arab civilization *in toto*, an undertaking that hinged on a strong Arab identity. Perhaps he thought his Palestinian identity would be thrown into question if it were revealed that he had not been born there. Until those who know the story's missing details come forward with the facts, we will never know why Jabra failed to mention his birth in Adana and his family's immigration to Bethlehem when he was a child. The answer may have been located somewhere in the personal papers, letters, diaries and books that filled Jabra's Baghdad library, but, as with the Yasser family papers in this novel, they were destroyed in a fiery explosion, erasing many records of his past.

Cry in a Long Night is the first truly modern Palestinian novel. One critic has called it the first 'artistically compelling' one, for its mature narrative techniques changed the course of modern Arabic literature. *Cry* is also an intimate, semi-autobiographical product of a man who wore many different hats: Jabra was a pioneering Palestinian modernist who helped wrench Arabic literature from the morass of Naturalism; a Syriac Orthodox convert to Sunni Islam; a Syriac refugee in Palestine and a Palestinian exile in Iraq; an erudite, Cambridge-educated Anglophile not unlike Nabokov or Borges; a meticulous autobiographer with a closet full of skeletons; a mid-century Wastelander (to use Saul Bellow's term); a man worried deeply about the future of Palestine and the Arab world; and a man caught between the nationalisms, modernisms, and genocides of the twentieth century.

William Tamplin
Somerville, Massachusetts
March 2021

Note on Transliteration

In line with Jabra's lifelong practice, I've tried to make the Arabic names in this book approachable and pronounceable for Anglophone readers unfamiliar with Arabic. For example, I've rendered Sumaya for 'Sumayyah' (the 'correct' transliteration), Samaa for 'Sammā',' and Shanoub for 'Shannūb.' Where common equivalents exist – like Yasser for Yāsir or Bethlehem for 'Bayt-laḥm' – I've used them. Following Jabra's example, I've sometimes used apostrophes, as in the name Khati'ah (*Khaṭī'ah*) in the short story 'Arak'. I've kept certain monetary denominations, like fils, dirhams and dinars, as well as the Turkish honorary titles 'Hanem' for 'Ms./Mrs.' or 'Lady,' and 'Pasha' for 'Mr.' or 'Sir,' and the Arabic paedonymics 'Umm' for 'mother of' and 'Abu' for 'father of.'

Chapter One

The young woman raised her foot and said, 'Look!' So I looked. But nothing about her foot interested me, except maybe her big toe, its nail painted red and protruding from the end of her elegant shoe. 'I'll proceed to something more fit for a man,' I told myself. And I headed towards the city.

On the way, I came across a rifle-toting policeman who stopped me to check my identity card. He turned out to be an old friend I'd once vacationed with on the mountain! His face looked exhausted, and his voice had lost its familiar vitality. 'I really am fed up with this work,' he said, as he patted me on the shoulder, leaving me perplexed, almost disappointed. I turned back towards him and called out, inviting him for a cup of coffee in the cafe nearby. But without looking back, he answered that he couldn't because he was still on the damned beat.

In the cafe, I came across the owner, Abu Hamed, whose head drooped drowsily upon his chest among the chairs and tables. He awoke suddenly at the chair's screech as I dragged it from a table. He came towards me, smiling and cheerful; he recognized me. He said that a lady from the Yasser family, whose name he couldn't exactly remember, had left me a telephone message, saying she wanted to see me that night – if that wasn't inconvenient for me – to discuss something, something Abu Hamed had forgotten.

I said to myself, 'God bless you and keep you, Inayat Hanem, but why don't you leave me alone?' I thanked the old man – Abu Hamed was around seventy – for his message. Then he brought me the coffee, and I savored it in that deserted place. How could I summon the energy at that hour to go to Inayat Yasser's palace, seeing as I'd just returned from a short vacation on the mountain, where I'd forgotten everything about her? I wasn't in a mental state fit for working, and I felt nothing but hate towards the city whose length I'd have to cross before arriving at her house. But I hoped to find her sister Roxane there. Seeing her was all ease and joy.

I set out.

To collect my scattered resolution, I lit a cigarette and took two deep drags. Then I cast it from me and watched the sparks fly from it. Suddenly a man – a beggar, no doubt – jumped out of the folds of the darkness, picked it up, and presently stuck it between his lips. I grinned and thought about giving him an entire cigarette, but chided myself for such softness and continued walking. On the road there were cars from which you could sometimes hear the sound of laughter, reminding you that there still were people in this world who took pleasure in life. That reminded me of Inayat Hanem, when she said she knew how to enjoy life, and of her hoarse, restrained laugh that would ring in my ears like a wincing moan or the cry of a jackal. (A few months before, we had spent a night in the village, which lies twenty kilometers from the city, in an ancient house overlooking a valley where the sad cries of jackals persisted throughout the night. I was astonished that Inayat Hanem not only found them annoying but was so afraid that she couldn't sleep.) She's probably waiting for me right now, and God only knows what family papers she's uncovered of late. Papers, papers, nothing but papers since I began working with her. Even though she paid me a good salary, I'd begun to tire of that kind of work. But work was work. I might also find Roxane there, and I liked talking to her. I found her affectionate towards me, too, and sometimes I suspected that she sought to catch me in her snares. But it would have been difficult for any woman to do so. When it came to women, I had put on the attitude of one who scorns them until I had actually come to scorn them. I'd failed in my marriage, and I was certain that the fate of any other relationship with any other woman could only end in failure..

A man walked towards me and smiled, for he thought he recognized me. He approached me warmly – and I started!

– and he went to shake my right hand, saying, 'Where've you been…?' When I didn't respond to his warmth, he faltered and stuttered from embarrassment, realizing that he had mistaken me for someone else. He began repeating, 'Pardon me, pardon me. I thought you were…' But I didn't linger to hear the rest of his explanation, and it struck me that I must resemble another man. 'It was the darkness, of course,' I told myself. I lit another cigarette. After I passed the street lamp, I examined my long shadow, which exaggerated the swing of my arm and betrayed a certain swagger in my gait. I rather liked the shape of my head as a shadow as it crept on ahead of me. But soon the shadow lengthened and lost its proportions, and I took no pleasure in studying it. I asked myself, 'Would I welcome an actual stranger if he struck up a conversation with me right now?'

The path was long and tortuous. My thoughts had overcome me, swarming about me like dozens of birds ever since I'd spent the last few days alone on vacation on the mountain, walking from place to place like a hermit with no companion but his staff. It seemed like those thoughts still followed me even in the streets of the city.

At a bend in the road, I saw a sign creaking gently in the wind with 'Shanoub Brothers – Branch Warehouse' written on it. I remembered how once I had gone there to meet Suleiman Shanoub, the first man who ever wanted to hire me. He was a stout man who wore thick, horn-rimmed glasses that magnified his small, piercing eyes. He greeted me with a smile that, as much as he tried, he couldn't make appear natural. While rubbing his smooth bald pate, he said, 'When you prove your worth, I'll promote you to clerk. But don't hurry. You have to be patient.' That day he made me open no fewer than fifty large boxes of toothpaste and scented soap in the warehouse basement. When I recalled that experience, I almost shuddered, imagining my fate had I returned to the warehouse the following morning. The strangest part was that I later married Suleiman Shanoub's own daughter. But our marriage didn't even last two years. The sign shook gently in the wind, and in its creaking I heard a laughing, a gloating derision I was powerless to respond to.

So I continued walking and approached the center of the city.

I told myself that Inayat Yasser was probably sitting in her library, sorting through the family letters, papers, documents, and the old memoirs whose pages had yellowed, whose ink had faded. When I arrived, she would press her cold, gaunt hand into mine in greeting, then present me with what she called 'a whole heap of new suggestions' and request that I 'study them' for a day or two. She had a ludicrous faith in the soundness of my judgment. Whenever her old clock struck midnight (and the last two strikes of the clock would always tarry such that I could laugh, if not for Inayat Hanem's adherence to extreme politeness), she would say in her familiar way, 'The day has come to an end, and the time for rest has arrived. Isn't that so, Mr. Amin?'

How I wished I could have asked her, 'And how is one to find rest, if you please?' But I refrained, for I knew she would think I was mocking her with my question. Afterwards I would almost always return to my house on foot. I usually wouldn't get home before one o'clock in the morning, and then I'd throw myself on my bed, my powers exhausted, and perhaps sleep. If I woke up early in the morning, I'd stay in bed reading, or work on my latest novel. Then I'd go to the newspaper's editorial office, where I would spend most of the day writing articles. I was used to churning them out because, after many long years of such work, I knew exactly what the readers wanted.

As for my novel, I sought in it a way to revive my straightened spirits. So I made it a means of expressing what I wanted to say, and divided myself into many characters, each one of whom represented a different part of this soul, so full of contradictions. I constructed the novel upon my love for Sumaya, the business owner's daughter – that love which failed to bear good fruit. But one doesn't always judge things by their fruit, or at least I didn't. Perhaps I hadn't been discerning enough in my approach: I used to insist upon the importance of experiencing life itself, heedless of the consequences.

That was a theory I had formed for my own peace of mind. After I suffered for a while, I tried to stake out a position towards life in which profit and loss, possession and poverty, would offset one another, and in which each opposed term would have a correspondent purpose and an equal value in the life of the individual. But I had to find the point at which the contradictions canceled each other out, and the manner in which the colors, in shades of both light and dark, could be arranged harmoniously. So I told myself I'd do that through writing. I would distribute bits and pieces of my experiences within the framework of a novel such that it would take, in the end, a form in which everything would fall into place and the parts would emphasize the beauty of the whole.

Inayat didn't know anything about my life. She was too preoccupied with the lives of her ancestors and their biographies for anything else – the very same biographies she and I were trying to distill from their letters, their memoirs, documents, and expense lists. On many occasions, I was forced to stifle a gloating laugh in my throat, caused by the pomposity of those venerable ancestors as they flaunted their silken clothes and feathered turbans before the eyes of the rabble, only to withdraw to their homes and try to seduce one of the village girls in their employ. Inayat Hanem would record every observation with amazing seriousness, and I had to follow her example. So I would record the date of the event, its principal details, and what she called 'the moral of the story.'

'The moral of the story!'

I was turning at a bend in the road when I spied a domestic

scene in a basement room with a window that gave onto the sidewalk. The window had no blinds, and an intense light poured from it, casting its iron bars' long shadows onto the road. I couldn't turn away from what was happening inside, for the sight captured my attention in spite of myself. I saw a man – a little over thirty – in his shirt, stuffing clothes into a suitcase lying open atop an iron bed frame. An old woman – perhaps his mother – was imploring him to stay (or so I gathered), while two other men stood in a corner of the room yelling at him to get the hell out. Shattered plates lay on the floor and a small black cat looked confusedly at the man packing. After I passed the window, their angry cries still filled the street, and an empty echo resounded among the large stone houses covered in darkness.

Such a sight wasn't unfamiliar to me. I'd witnessed innumerable scenes of fights; scenes overflowing with curses and blows. Sometimes a mother would erupt in a fit of anger and with the ferocity of a wolf attacked her son with her shoes, or the neighbors would explode into a petty squabble that gathered sons and daughters alike in its grasp, the cause nothing but a squalid toilet blackened by cobwebs. I knew the city inside and out, but before I was delivered of the net of poverty that my family had suffered for centuries, I myself had participated in a large part of the city's battles and had smelled a liberal share of its stench. I had also known its spontaneous joys and the rabble's raucous laughs. But in the house of the business owner Shanoub, I'd had to plunge into a scene of repugnance and disgust the likes of which I hadn't known in the poor quarters.

One day Sumaya came to me and insisted that I go to her father and ask him for her hand, as tradition required. Because the matter of our marrying had aroused a great deal of argument and aversion between father and daughter, I was wary of paying him a visit before being absolutely certain that it would lead to the realization of our desire to marry. Thus she came to inform me that she had won the battle after great difficulty, and I had only to go to her father to win her hand.

I ascended the wide staircase of her enormous house, and she greeted me at the door in a yellow blouse and a green skirt, for she knew that I loved those two colors on her. She pressed my hand and whispered that everything was fine. Then she led me to the living room and left me with the promise that she would return a minute later. I immediately noticed a number of dreadful oil paintings unworthy of their frames hanging on the walls. But I was delighted to see the beautiful Persian rug that covered the floor of the entire room, and the view of the city from the windows soothed the eye. The city looked as beautiful as it could have: large white houses embellishing a vast tapestry of trees and flowers.

Yet my nerves were on edge. I looked around furtively and inhaled the scent of wealth. I couldn't ignore the fact that the air wasn't totally pure; nevertheless, my presence in an enormous, multi-roomed house with an elegant marble staircase (how I wished there had been a statue at its top!) gave me the impression that the air was cold and pure. I searched my pockets for cigarettes, lit one, and sat smoking, guardedly, in a comfortable chair. Perhaps the smoke would calm my nerves.

Sumaya returned agitated. 'What happened?' I asked.

'I don't know,' she said. 'My father, he's not reliable. Right now he's in the bathroom shaving, and he'll be here as soon as he's done. He wasn't pleased that I invited you over while my mother was out. Even though that was what he suggested.'

Then she approached me and gave me a quick kiss. When I offered her a cigarette, she refused it and sat down at the piano. She didn't play well, but I felt that any music at that moment, however it was played, would ease the intensity of the crisis. Yet the atmosphere remained tense.

After a while, her father came in, his lips wearing the same smile he'd flashed me years ago when he'd wanted to hire me. His head looked larger and balder than it had before, his eyes more penetrating, the horn-rimmeds thicker.

When we shook hands, I charged mine with all the warmth I could muster; Sumaya regarded us with obvious concern.

Right away, as he eased down into his chair, he said, 'Mr. Amin, I'm very pleased to welcome you here in our home.

I've heard a lot about you from Sumaya. No doubt I'll find a good friend in you.'

'Of course, of course!' Sumaya cried out.

He shot her a cursory glance. Then he directed his penetrating eyes towards me and said with total composure, 'I think you've been in love with each other for a while now. Is that not so?'

'Yes, sir,' I said. 'That's why I've come here – to have the honor of paying you a visit, and to ask for Sumaya's hand.'

'Sumaya told me as much.'

'I hope you'll grant us your approval.'

But he didn't respond, only saying, 'Do you consider yourself one of the new generation of youth, fond of adventure and risk-taking? Because I only like risk-takers, those who embark fearlessly upon the new.' Before I could respond, he added, 'And there's no one I hate more than the content failure of a man. Do you consider yourself a success or a failure in life?'

His sermonizing bothered me, but I answered him, saying, 'Seeing as I started from nothing, you could consider me a success. But I'm still at the beginning of the race.'

'Of course, of course. Ah…here, Umm Sumaya has just arrived.'

A tall woman with a pudgy face entered, still panting from ascending the stairs. Her large hand – as if one were looking at it from behind a magnifying glass – held an ugly leather bag, swollen from its contents. I noticed Sumaya leap from her seat in alarm, for we hadn't been expecting her at that hour.

She shouted at her daughter, saying, 'Is that your fiancé, Sumaya?'

When I stood up to shake her hand, my heart sank. She had apparently decided to insult me as much as she could because she ignored my extended right hand and said, 'Listen, Amin, there's no need to waste time. We won't let you destroy our daughter's future. Take it from me in one simple phrase: We will never consent to your marriage, and there's no use in beating around the bush. And you,' she said as she turned to Sumaya, leaning on the piano, her mouth agape, 'isn't it shameful, what you're doing? What will people say about us?'

'But Mamma,' Sumaya said, 'weren't we finished with that kind of talk?'

'How could we be finished with it while you still insist on acting at your own discretion? Was it for this occasion that we raised you, that we spent money on your education, your edification? So you could bring home a man like this, a man whose ancestry and background no one even knows, and insist on marrying him? What will people say about us?'

I stood there to receive the stream of her insults. I felt I was sinking bit by bit into a swamp comprised of everything loathsome to the soul. I noticed that the oil paintings were looking doltishly at us from the walls. In his chair, Suleiman

Shanoub had been transformed into a despicable, deformed imp while his wife looked like a gargoyle scowling from above a basin, spewing sewage from its mouth.

Sumaya blanched and said, trembling, 'What do I care what people say as long as I marry the man I love?'

'Shut up, you shameless girl!' her father yelled.

'I love him,' she yelled back, 'I love him, and no one will stand between us!' And she fell into her chair.

As for me, I headed towards the door without knowing exactly how to escape the situation. When I reached the door, I said, 'Your daughter's given you our answer, Umm Sumaya. I don't think you'll be able to stop us from getting married.'

Umm Sumaya struck her cheek and said, 'For shame!'

'How could my marriage possibly bring shame upon your highborn family and blue blood?' I asked.

'That's something you wouldn't understand, you little street rat!' she responded.

'I ask the Lord, ma'am, not to bestow upon me such majesty as yours, the source of which is a toothpaste warehouse. And I ask the Lord to pour into the pipes of this city enough water to cleanse myself of your family's soap suds – that fount of nobility and prestige! Sumaya! Are you staying?'

'Please leave,' muttered the despicable deformed imp from the depths of his chair.

Sumaya looked at me from behind a veil of tears like a kitten playing fierce. 'I'm going with Amin,' she yelled.

'Go at your own risk!' her mother said. 'I swear to God, we'll disown you!'

'I don't want anything from you,' Sumaya bellowed. 'Not money, not servants, not stores. It's all yours. Enjoy it!'

Suddenly the little imp stood up and landed a slap on her cheek – his glasses nearly falling off his face – but she didn't budge. 'What do you two know about life, living here in such disgusting luxury?' she said. 'Come on, Amin. There's nothing for us to do except leave.'

She took my arm, pulled me out of the room, and slammed the door violently behind her. 'I'm going to pack some clothes,' she said, 'and I'll come back down right away. Wait.'

When I descended the marble staircase, I realized why there wasn't a statue at the top, and I understood the reason for the ugly oil paintings. But I also understood that I had assumed for myself a responsibility requiring more courage than I'd expected. When Sumaya came down with her small bag and embraced me, my head was surging with the sounds of rage, wrath and wretchedness. But soon enough the elation of victory washed over us like a tidal wave. When a taxi took us to my small house, I told myself I'd give the driver a large tip, and so I did. I carried Sumaya in my arms from the garden gate to the door of the house, and then directly to bed. Then all of a sudden, my head was rushing with the sounds of laughter and crazed joy, and I cried out at the top of my voice, 'What woman in this world has a body this beautiful?'

Chapter Two

I remembered everything clearly and described it all in detail in my novel. But now I felt I'd made the matter into a melodrama fatuous on more than a few levels. Sumaya was, of course, a beautiful young woman: Does a young woman *not* leave an everlasting impression in the mind of a man if he considers her the most beautiful of God's creatures?

We first met in a forest about fifteen kilometers from the city, on one of those mercurial March days that begins clear and warm and ends thunderous and stormy. I'd ridden my bicycle to the village, my birthplace and childhood stomping ground. In the course of my return, the sky darkened suddenly, winds raged, and rain poured. As soon as I neared the forest, I took shelter under the trees while the storm abated. There was a young woman there with her bicycle, stirring up my sympathy with her wet clothes and her moist, matted hair.

I stood my bicycle against a tree and asked her, 'Is the damsel in distress?'

'Yes, and I'm soaked through, too!' she responded.

'Don't you have a jacket?'

'Who thought it was going to rain like this?'

'I know, it's outrageous. And it doesn't look like it's going to stop anytime soon.'

Thunder crashed unexpectedly, and the young woman started. Then she said, with a look of fear in her eyes, 'We shouldn't stand under the trees. Lightning's dangerous – it could strike us at any moment.'

'Lightning strike or no lightning strike, I'll wait here until the rain stops. I've ridden my bicycle more than twenty kilometers this morning, and a little rest wouldn't hurt. But you're trembling. Did you get very wet?'

'Very. I rode my bike to the old bridge, and suddenly the clouds thickened. So I turned back, but it was too late. At first, I didn't dare take cover under the trees for fear of the lightning. I thought I could reach home before the rain tired me out. And you see what kind of state I'm in now! So I had to stop here.'

'All right, very well,' I said. It was delightful to find her there, a strange unknown woman. 'Whatever happens, I prefer a possible lightning strike to a definite case of bronchitis.'

Her body shivered distinctly and she said, 'God knows, if

I escape one, I won't escape the other.'

'Go easy on yourself. And smile a little. Shall I give you my jacket?'

When I put my jacket over her shoulders, a gust of wind shook a spray of raindrops from the leaves onto our heads.

I got out my cigarettes and said, 'Do you smoke?'

'No. But I will now.'

The wisps of smoke began twisting from between her lips in total silence. We listened intently to the raindrops' patter upon the leaves. *Leaves, papers, sheaves, leaves* – I said to myself – while the raindrops beat fast like a frightened heart. The thunder crashed again, and the young woman looked up in fright.

'Shall we go?' she asked.

'I don't know…where are you going?'

'To the city – to the western hill.'

Then I realized that she was definitely well-off.

'I have a small apartment in that part of the city,' I said. 'If you want, you could come home with me and dry yourself off…'

'You live alone? How lucky!'

'Who's to say?'

She looked at me and seemed to be smiling when she tossed her cigarette butt into a small pool of rainwater. I thought that if she trimmed her hair just a bit, she'd be a great deal more beautiful.

'I'm leaving!' she called out. 'I've gotten wetter than I can stand, and I'd like to go before I lose what little resolution I have left.'

'All right then. Let's go.'

When we mounted our bikes, her wheels skidded, but she immediately regained her balance. The rain hadn't let up, and she asked me, 'Do you want your jacket back?'

Relishing the role of the chivalrous knight, I said, 'No. The rain might stop soon.'

Into the wind she shouted, 'Optimist!'

Optimist! That's how she would later characterize me. I fell in love with her like a fool falling unprepared into a raging sea, my love crazy and desperate. She came to my two-room apartment with no insistence from me, and perhaps, in her exhaustion, she couldn't resist.

I ran a hot bath for her, and when she went into the bathroom and locked the door, I stripped my clothes off in the bedroom, dried myself off, and put on some clean clothes. I got out one of my shirts and a pair of gray pants for her to wear.

How marvelously transformed she was when she emerged in my clothes, her hair parted down the middle and its ends descending to her shoulders, silky and soft! 'Dear God!' I cried out. She smiled as she looked around the room.

'I won't forget this good deed of yours. I don't know why I came here. But here I am, and I'm happy to be here.'

'And now, how about something to eat? But first – what's your name?'

'Sumaya. Sumaya Suleiman Shanoub.'

'Suleiman Shanoub? That's incredible! I mean – I mean, I almost worked for your father once, many years ago. That is, if he's the owner of the well-known business.'

'The very same. And now, didn't you ask me about something to eat?'

She laughed.

Then I told her my name.

Chapter Three

Amin, Amin. She used to love repeating my name. She would press her lips against my cheek while uttering the first syllable, then raise them to pronounce the second, then the first, then the second... I'd begun to walk now, as if in a trance, my mind floating upon a stream of memories, and I repeated my name to myself, as if to recover the old intoxication. But the voice of Sumaya, which I'd imagined was calling me, evoked the ghost of my father from the dust of oblivion – from that forgetfulness with which love armed itself against my other life experiences. Love had practically effaced every trace left in my mind of my relatives and my many friends. Whenever a wave from the past overcame me, it came carrying various images of the same woman: as she caresses me and scolds me, entices me only to withdraw from me, surrenders to me and weeps, her eyes pressed to my face, then laughs and laughs as she seeps into my bloodstream. Whenever the past revealed my father calling out to me, Sumaya would appear, like a bystander at the edge of my brain observing what transpired within.

My father filled the days of my childhood with stories and songs. One thing that was a bit strange was Inayat Hanem's habit, during an hour of rest after hours of work, of asking me to tell her something about my father's life. She would compare him, whether consciously or not, to her own ancestors, even if no resemblance existed between a poor gardener and members of the perishing aristocracy. When she learned of my father's ability to improvise songs, she became interested because of certain theories of inspiration and poetry her grandfather had detailed in a book that remained in manuscript form in the family's large library.

That grandfather of hers – Izzeddine Yasser – was a poet, and much of his poetry was still worth reading. He was known for his mellifluous voice, set some of his poems to music, and sang them – but only to his kin and close friends. Despite his respect for music and musicians, he feared that the villagers who lived under his authority would learn of his singing and cease to respect him. Nevertheless, he would invite to his palace some musicians who had mastered the oud or qanoon, show them his new compositions, and sing to the accompaniment of their instruments. My father, however, would sing spurred on by an instinctual drive. He was invited to every wedding in the village, where everyone sang their throats out. Since my father was illiterate, he would improvise verses in the colloquial dialect – I could still recall many of them and marveled at their beauty – which the village folk would later transmit among themselves, so much so that they would forget the verses' source. If he were accompanied by a musical instrument, it would usually be a humble reed flute fashioned by a friend of his: My father would start singing, his friend would immediately pick up on the key and improvise his tunes and melodies to harmonize, and they would continue like that for as long as the Good Lord let them.

I was around four or five years old when one day my father called out to me, saying, 'Amin, I'm going to sing now, and you're going to dance!'

He held me between his large, open palms and began swaying me right and left to his song, turning me around and jumping me up and down, indicating the rhythm by the successive pressure of his hands on my hips until the rhythm began flowing into my body. I found myself dancing in my own way, rocking and turning amid my family's laughs and claps. When I stopped dancing and could have fallen to the floor from exhaustion, they all yelled, roaring with laughter and joy, 'Come on, Amin, come on, keep it going!' My father resumed his song, and still they hadn't stopped clapping, 'Keep it up, don't stop!' and I found myself tapping the floor to the rhythm, reeling and swaying, while the clamor of my name repeated filled my ears: 'Amin, Amin, Amin…'

That was the same verbal rhythm that rang in my ears whenever Sumaya clung to me in one of her drunken fits of passion, for she would say only, 'Amin, Amin, Amin…' Then we would dance in our small room, spinning fast in front of the mirror, and then, with rhythmic steps, glide into the back garden and fall, worn out, upon the grass.

Chapter Four

I had already begun walking more slowly when I found myself looking at an illuminated sign that read, 'Garden Cafe.' It was a place I patronized often. Since I wasn't eager to see Inayat Hanem immediately, I thought about sitting for a while in the cafe, getting a drink and chatting with some friends I might find there. One had to plunge into a tight, dark alley that stank with heaps of garbage and then turn right behind a gate made of iron rings and bars in order to glimpse a garden with iron tables and chairs in the midst of a quarter that a few huge buildings had turned their backs on. In the daytime, if you were a new customer, you couldn't rid your mind of the water pipes and sewage lines that scarred the backs of those towering buildings. But at night, when most of the windows overlooking the cafe were illuminated, you could forget the pipes and see the shapes of many people looking out the windows in pairs.

If not for two women sitting in a corner of the cafe, the place would have been empty. There was a radio playing faint music, and when I sat down at one of the tables, I recalled those long afternoons and evenings that Sumaya and I had spent in abandon as we played our favorite records. Our feelings changed and transformed according to the harshness or delicacy of the melody like the movements of a dancer. In our garden we had roses – some red, some yellow. We preferred the yellow ones because, as we used to say, they reflected the sun's blaze, the fire of life. Sometimes, after a downpour, the sun would burst forth in opulent colors from between the clouds, pouring through the double window onto the couch where Sumaya lay, seductive in her semi-nudity, her breasts bare in that golden glow. Music would gush from the gramophone like a stream of lovers' fantasies, and I would say *Those streams contained white geese flying and boats floating drowsily*, and she'd say *No, those are ghosts sailing across the seas to cast their anchors upon the shores of Dance*, or that perhaps *They were demons expelled by the eddies of Hell*. Sometimes the music contained the calm of the countryside in summer, when all nature quiets down save the grasshoppers and the flies. I'd sit across from Sumaya and, never tired or bored, look at her as she pretended to read. I'd say to her, in endless expressions of love, that her hair was like a wheat field before the harvest, that on its sides hung yellow flowers, that her eyes were thus, and her lips thus, analyzing her body part by part in order to ascribe to it the most perfect beauty God had created for man's pleasure. The trees would sway outside in the sun, and Sumaya would move an arm and turn a page in her book, and I'd change how I was sitting to better adjust the gramophone and exhaust my mind in search of similes and metaphors. Then she would get up to tell me that she loves me with her body, for her body was a part of the sun and a gift from it, and she would place the ripeness of her body between my arms until the sun sank behind the far hills and the clouds gathered in the western horizon. The pitter-patter of a golden sleep would steal over our bodies. I would wake up hours later to find that her tears had moistened my cheek, as if a sadness were tossing her about, a sadness she was incapable of describing. Then I'd be assailed by worry about that obscure yearning tormenting her, and I'd feel that it, despite her love for me, was taking her away from me.

While I was sitting and waiting for the waiter to arrive, three men and a woman entered. They chose a table near the two women who, I realized, were among the cafe's *frequent patrons*; their ugliness was pitiful. I immediately recognized them, but I hesitated to approach. One of them, Rashid Boutros, was an old friend who had begun to annoy me of late with his pedantry and his loud, shrill voice. His wife Dania annoyed me no less because of a passion that had once sprung up between us in which she only surrendered to me after I'd grown tired of seeing her face. As for the other two men, they were friends whose company I never tired of. One of them, Fares al-Tibi, styled himself an artist, even if he hadn't produced more than fifteen paintings in his life. But no one held that against him due to his friendliness, good company and conversation. The other, Omar al-Sameri, was a truly wondrous young man; he had excelled in his studies, graduated from college before he turned twenty, and for two years traveled extensively throughout the Arab countries and part of Europe. He then returned to the city as a beautiful symbol of sarcasm and ennui. He had the face of an angel and the tongue of a devil. Though he was beloved equally of men and women, in his view, human affection was all absurdity and folly. Nothing in life interested him other than what he called 'the hell of the alley.' Since he had all the ease and luxury that one could desire, he found no mental stimulation in anything save the misfortune and misery of others.

I couldn't hesitate for long. Firstly, because I hadn't seen Fares and Omar in a long time; then, because I didn't want to remain a haunted man with Sumaya's ghost pursuing me mercilessly. So I got up and walked between the chairs in their direction. Omar saw me before anyone else and yelled, 'Here comes Amin Samaa bearing the visage of Christ! Where have you been hiding all this time?'

'In a cave on the mountain.'

'With the foxes and jackals, no doubt?' Rashid asked.

'With choirs of angels,' Fares said, correcting him. 'Who

but angels would live in the tower of Amin, *faithful and true*?'

I laughed and said, 'It's more like a castle of clay, *in the dirt and the dew*.'

The waiter came, and we ordered glasses of beer.

'And what hymn were the angels singing?' Omar asked me.

'They were praising mercenary writing for the newspapers,' I responded.

'Mercenary writing for the newspapers?' Omar said. 'I've tried it. There's no good in it and no fun. You don't cheer up the masses, and you don't even make yourself happy. And when you do make some money, chances are you'll spend it on the most trivial of things. That's why I'd prefer to pick my nose.'

'How about picking *my* nose, for a change?' Fares said with an earnest tone. 'It's our duty to take turns picking each other's noses. Amin, you must write to your readers about this grave matter. You must prepare a series of articles entitled 'Pick Your Neighbor's Nose.' I'm prepared to illustrate it for you so the readers understand it and its meaning isn't lost on anyone.'

'That's an adolescent pursuit,' Rashid said. 'As for those who've reached the age of reason, *sinn al-rushd*...'

Fares interrupted him, 'You mean the Rashidians, the Mature Ones, after your own name.'

'Yes!' Rashid laughed. 'As for the Rashidians, they must be taught virtues more elevated than that. Instruct them, for example, on how to slap the asses of their neighbors' wives without making any noise. Lots of people find pleasure in that, in addition to learning.'

'That reminds me of Fares' latest painting,' Omar said. 'Have you seen it, Amin? It's Fares' desire, just like it's no doubt the desire of many other people, among whom I count myself – anyway, I was saying that Fares' soul longs for women's asses. In that respect, he's like the Flemish painter Rubens, except that Fares here prefers the rest of a woman's body to be slender and delicate. And we all agree on that too. The result of all that is that we crave a mix of classic beauty – the full and fleshy – and the beauty of movie stars, the sparkling, metallic glamor. Doesn't that mean we're in an age of transition, even in matters of taste? That's what I told Fares when I saw the painting he calls *Woman in a Mirror*, with her slender body, small breasts, and her enormous derriere. There's something almost bovine about it. Still though, it tempts the sensual hand to reach out and touch it...you really must see it, Amin.'

'Of course, naturally,' I said. I turned towards Fares and asked him, 'Have you seriously gone back to painting, then?'

'Two days ago I began painting a woman with her child,' he said. 'A woman with her child, imagine that!'

'Does that speak to your longing for married life?' I asked.

'Till now, I haven't known such a longing,' he said. 'For me, Woman is a collection of lines and cubes, brushstrokes and blocks. That's why I love her body. But I wouldn't pay two pennies for her mind. And that's why I couldn't imagine living with one.'

Dania protested, saying, 'That only speaks to your despair, Fares. Surely numerous women have rejected you despite your love for them, so you've begun justifying your attachment to them by limiting your interest to their bodies. That is, you've begun to fear romantic entanglements. And that only means that you're fleeing from reality.'

'My dear Dania,' I said, 'I have no doubt that Fares is treating Woman just how she deserves. If men limit their interest to women's bodies, as opposed to their minds, they're only repaying them in kind, for women don't see anything in men save *their* bodies. A woman is a lump of sensitive flesh; that's why touching her is all pleasure. And women, by virtue of their sex, wear clothes of various colors. Her figure has more curves than Man's; that's why painting her is also pleasurable. But romantic entanglements are artificial, even if traditions of marriage solidify them. Passion for men is explosive, irregular – it doesn't follow him like his shadow. For him, his body doesn't take up more than a bit of his time. But for a woman, her body is everything. She bathes it, perfumes it, paints it with all kinds of makeup, exposes its various parts, and carries it with her wherever she goes like precious cargo, all in order to eventually lay it down in the bed of some man. There's no end to it, even if the body becomes wrinkled and flabby and unsuitable for the bed. The passion rooted deep within it is an unsatisfiable craving.'

My head was rushing with the words of Sumaya, whose lies and duplicity became apparent to me in the end. I certainly didn't think that lovers' dreams lasted forever, but Sumaya destroyed the dream with a surprise betrayal, and I opened my eyes to find myself on the edge of the abyss. Despite all that, images of lush femininity flashed before my eyes as I spoke, and my words wrapped themselves around wondrously sculpted limbs before they reached my lips. Dania had shrunk in my regard to a loathsome sort of thing, and I couldn't stand to look at her. But her husband encircled her waist with his arm and said, 'Poor Amin. You talk like a stung man.'

I looked at him and laughed, and Dania understood the reason for my laughter. For in that situation and setting, he was the quintessence of self-important matrimony, oblivious that Dania didn't miss a chance to fall in love on the side and that her adulterous nature had cast her into many unpleasant relationships. So I just laughed and said nothing.

'It's clear that this emphasis on the body is the result of technological or financial progress,' Omar said. 'For example, in a country like America, where women use electronic appliances, LP gas and chrome-plated tools for their household chores – women there discover they have excess leisure time to fill. And with us, when the servants take care of all the cooking and cleaning, rich women find themselves in a similar position with regard to leisure. But her leisure time is much vaster than her Western sister's. Leisure is the enemy of God. It's an appendage of riches and progress. And only rarely does spiritual development accompany progress or riches. The body is the eternal factor in human existence, with all its passions, each one of them a voracious maw. And when all these passions are satisfied, the sexual passion remains, ever ready to explode, under the repression of many long centuries. Men with leisure time in this age of ours could split their time between sex and rational thinking. As for women, I don't think they'll apply themselves to anything save trying on different sexual masks. Much of what fills her life – makeup, color magazines – is just a stand-in for sex. Just a body disguising itself anew every day.'

'And what's the harm in that?' Fares asked. 'We've had enough of the Dark Ages, when the body was considered an enemy to man. It's time for us to make the spirit our enemy. And if technological advancement emphasizes the body, then I'm all for it. I simply cannot stand anything that's backward or underdeveloped. Wherever man lacks for technological advancement, he finds poverty and filth. And man's struggle against poverty diverts him from his body, save its instinctual and animalistic natures. So he covers his struggle with a robe of spirituality, he glorifies his poverty with religious phrases, and he dies in the end the death of an animal – from effort and exhaustion, without knowing the minutiae of feeling and pleasure.'

Rashid began stroking his wife's neck, running his fingers over her cheeks, lips and hair.

So I said, directing my speech first and foremost to Fares, 'You're conflating culture with progress, the refinement of sensibility with money. If progress, with all its machines and inventions, grants us vast amounts of time to care for the body, then what I fear is that said care won't be anything but negative, such that man will demand external pleasure and will be subservient to it, without putting his own talents to use, until he's struck by that terrible sickness: ennui. Ennui, for its part, ruins the body, and man then falls into a vicious circle. When he feels he has everything he desires, but nothing makes him happy, then that odious question repeats on his tongue: What should I do now? For he'll say: I'm fed up with drinking, I'm fed up with books, I'm fed up with women, I'm fed up with movies, I'm fed up with this music flowing from the radio…and the list goes on. What's the meaning of all that, if not that his life has become empty of the bodily response – the muscular response – to the phenomena of nature? Because it's the hand that creates! Whether its creation is a ditch, or an apple tree, or a statue – it's raw, muscular creation. Such creation is man's only savior. But in the 'advanced' world, it's clear that that kind of work is limited to the 'backward' segments in every country: the villages. And the poor and the lower classes. Because if they don't work, they die. The hand that presses electronic buttons in houses full of servants – it's forgotten the need to create. The best it can do, in an atmosphere of intellectual, scientific and artistic enlightenment, is to distinguish between the pleasurable sensations. The worst it can do is go about groping thighs or, when necessary, using the revolver. That's why I think the villages and the lower classes of people produce the vast majority of artists and creators in the cities, even if their names aren't known. But people of leisure, those who enjoy the fruits of progress, they're a breeding ground of ennui and disgust.'

I didn't wish to mention then that my father, a gardener at the monastery in our village, hadn't used the word 'ennui' at all. Perhaps he didn't even know the word existed. My father was part of the seasons: the spring with its flowers and songs, the summer with its harvests and lusts, the fall with its olives and weddings, and the winter with its bitter cold and expectations. What idle talk city folk go spouting as they discuss the delights of the body! They don't know a tenth of those delights! They lost what little they had of spiritual resolution and then lost their bodily vitality, and the only thing they have left is the mere dregs of their energy when compared to the sons of the villages and certain poor folk. In addition to what the latter possess in terms of muscular activity, they could, when they think about God, almost reach the heights of religious ecstasy. I remember how my father would rise from his bed every Sunday morning at four and go to the priest's house to wake him so that he could begin prayers in the church at five. Prayers would last two or three hours, and my father would enjoy every word recited. To him, 'the spirit' was something real, not merely an obscure word. He believed in another world, a heavenly bounty that the human mind could not comprehend. When I was eight years old, he said to me, 'Amin, if you listen closely to the word of God, you'll find the world bursting with joy.' But he died when I was ten, and we had to move to the city like refugees, with no one to provide for us except my older brother, who worked as a mechanic in the city. Thus we abandoned the hills, valleys and vineyards for the dark quarter, with its grave-like houses, overflowing toilets, and polluted air. I witnessed 'progress' from below, if I can put it that way. I witnessed it as a stranger to it, and then as a victim of it. What kind of progress are they talking about?! What knowledge of the delights of the senses?! After I spent my years reading books by the light of an oil lamp – sleeping the first part of the night, then waking in the wee hours after midnight, as the neighborhood slumbered, to return to the oil lamp and my reading – and after I saw the books I'd written sell, and the doors of society opening in my face, I didn't encounter even ten men or women who asked themselves seriously about human life or its mental or sensual needs.

While Omar began speaking about that subject in his

idiosyncratic way, the city lay exposed before my eyes, reduced to the smallest of its forms: wealthy people reclining in huge cars, youth with emaciated bodies lurking in the corners preparing for a lethal attack, ladies wrapped in furs, women with wrinkled faces leading children clinging to the hems of their tattered robes.

Starting from where I left off, Omar said, 'People of leisure, those who enjoy the fruits of progress – I know every last one of them. I've known leisure with its gaping maw to devour them time after time. The only way they know how to escape it is through eating, screwing or gambling. But I found myself a way out of that life of theirs when I discovered that the sweetest thing in life is the contemplation of misery and need and everything that emanates from them. I do admit that I was too much of a coward for one thing: to live in one of those soiled, unkempt alleys immersed in a terrifying fog from the stench of the sewers. But I've long dreamt of that, and perhaps my dream will shortly be realized.'

'Didn't you find anything else, anything with a sweeter air?' Rashid asked him.

'Yes,' he responded. 'I discovered that all women sweat in their armpits, and that the most beautiful creature under the sun has to concern herself with the movement of her bowels, which makes toilets an inescapable necessity. Are you laughing? This is a grave matter, as long as we're speaking about the body. All I know about the body is this: It's the source of all squalor. Wherever people are found, so are bedbugs and flies. So if you love the body, you have to love all that comes with it. And if you want to know more, then read that rebellious Frenchman guffawing his way down the centuries, Rabelais. I don't believe in anything except Rabelais.'

Rashid said, not knowing whether Omar was in earnest or in jest, 'As for me, I believe in Dania. You all are entitled to picking your noses or the noses of others, and you're entitled to wallowing in manure if you so desire. As for me, I have my wife. And she won't inspire me with such thoughts of yours, and thank God for that. Listen, Omar. You need a little wife to worship you. She'll cure you of this despairing deviance, she'll elevate your mind…'

'God forbid!' Omar yelled. 'Who wants an elevated mind? Perhaps one could wish for a broad mind or a deep mind. But an elevated mind…that's a kind of arrogance that I won't accept, Rashid. You're entitled to love Dania – don't we all love you, Dania? – but you're going too far with this blather when you talk about the *elevated mind.*'

Fares emerged from between the folds of his calm and said, 'I've got an idea, everyone! How about I add a spider or a black cockroach to the painting *Woman in a Mirror*? A huge black cockroach.'

Dania shook her head, saying, 'Disgusting!'

But Omar called out, 'Great idea! *Woman in Mirror with Black Cockroach Between Her Breasts*…an amazing title!'

'Truly disgusting,' Dania said. 'Aren't her two huge ugly buttocks enough for you?'

'Put the cockroach on her butt,' I suggested. 'And the painting's message will be, just like Omar says, that our beauty is soiled with our deviance.'

'Wonderful, wonderful!' Omar added, as a boisterous guffaw escaped his throat.

'You're all disregarding what man admires,' Rashid said, 'and you don't perceive anything save imperfection and crookedness. Then you add insult to injury with your inverted logic, your denial of true, correct values, and your creation of these paintings as if they're nightmares. There's no doubt your minds are the playgrounds of cockroaches. When you contemplate the love of a woman, you don't find pleasure in anything except cracking jokes about her ass. You think people are scoundrels if they're rich and beggars if they're poor. You detest chastity and virtue but attack whatever isn't chaste and virtuous. As for your views on women, they're either cheap whores or they suck men's blood. Do you know what you should add to your painting, Fares? A bunch of leeches in the woman's hands. So that its message will become: *Thus does she suck the blood of men*. While you sit here and formulate everything according to your direct perception of all the ugliness and vulgarity that surrounds you, aren't you ignoring other aspects of city life? Why should man get bored when he has music, films, exhibitions, museums, clean houses, colleges, gardens, parties, perfumes, flowers and everything else? I'm afraid you're sick in your delusions. I'm well aware of your love for beautiful things, of your wide acquaintance with culture. But your minds are infected. And none of that will serve you.'

I said to myself that Rashid, even if he exaggerated the importance of what we were about, had hit the nail on the head for the first time in his life. Our despair grew deeper day after day without our understanding it precisely. That said, it was a kind of despair that had its roots in the soul of each one of us, even if we weren't able to dissect and analyze it with precision. Take my own despair, for example. As soon as I managed to weave together the life of the mind with that of the senses, to enjoy the diversity and munificence that existence has arranged for us, the calm and contentment of my life was torn apart by the disappearance of Sumaya. Her disappearance was, at least, what occasioned those black currents of despair and bitterness to gush forth only to drag me with them. And I was only twenty-six years old.

After I spent my teenage years occupied with words, writing something every day, no matter how trifling, I wrote two books, and the miracle occurred. In the blink of an eye, I became an object of conversation and discussion, an object of slander and praise, and I realized that that was the beginning of fame. The miracle continued, and suddenly the two books came out in a second edition. I came upon a little money, dreamed widely, and said I would leave poverty behind forever…and my head was full of ideas for new books. When I met Sumaya and fell in love, I found in her admiration and encouragement an incentive for me to keep rushing forward. In reality, I wasn't but a child, and my knowledge of life anywhere, save the neighborhood where I lived, was only vague and fragmented. Yet in my soul was the faith and fervor of a child, and love filled me with confidence and pride. After that rainy day, which announced the beginning of change in my life, Sumaya would sneak over to my little house because she hadn't told her parents about me. She would recline with her beautiful, statuesque figure on the couch and talk about her childhood. I'd see the enormous gap between her childhood in the city under the wing of two parents with a measure of wealth, and my childhood in the village or in the old neighborhood.

Once I told her, 'When I was a small boy in the village, a rainy night descended upon us, like – as I recall it now – like it was one of the decisive nights of world history. The rain poured incessantly, in buckets, throughout the hours of darkness, and I curled up in my pallet bed, stretched out on the floor, in search of warmth. But the windows and the many cracks in the walls (which in the summer made the house well ventilated) began to suck the cold wind inside, and it penetrated our blankets to caress our poor joints! I couldn't sleep, so I got up and piled on top of my blanket every piece of cloth or clothing that my hands fell upon in the darkness. But instead of their warmth, I felt only their weight. In the sheep pen – separated from our room by only an unhinged door – three lambs were sneezing and bleating in fear, and I began wondering whether they also felt the cold, whether they would get sick and die and dash our hopes for the tiny profit we were counting on from selling them. My mother had asked me to record an expense list for the lambs. She promised that if we made a big profit, she wouldn't take me out of school to work in the fields. That's why I was so alarmed and disturbed that night, thinking I might be forced to leave school. The rain continued pouring and drumming on the door and windows while my father snored, enviable in his slumber. I couldn't keep warm, and I feared the sheep I had taken responsibility for would die, and that I would be forbidden from attending school.

'But in the end I fell asleep. When I awoke in the morning, I was weary from the weight of all the covers on my bed. I stood on the doorstep, shivering slightly because of the wind, which blew freezing and refreshing. I beheld the sky's blue surface, with transparent, cottony clouds scattered within it. Our yard had turned into a large pool that ducks now played in, every one of them beating its wings and dipping its head in the yellow water, and then paddling about in it free of worry and care. In the farthest horizon I saw the dome of the monastery shining like an arrow shooting out towards the cosmos.

'I said to my mother, 'God had mercy on us, the rains didn't do us any harm. And by the way, I'm hungry.' I asked her to prepare us some hot tea. But her first question was about the three sheep. I called out 'Ahh, the sheep! I forgot all about them!' I put on some clogs, went to the pen, and found the three animals alive, lying in each other's embrace. I told her that they were alive and well! Then I knew I would keep going to school.'

Sumaya would listen raptly and delightedly to such stories. She said she had never touched a sheep in her life. Then she would tell me something about her own life. Listening to her, I used to feel a kind of disappointment, and would wonder: If this were her spoiled and protected life, then how did she manage to find the source of life's poetry later on, when she revealed to me her excessive sensuality in the first months of our marriage? She was her parents' only child, so no wonder they spoiled her and infected her with their opinions on life and the world. She grew up with an unjustifiable arrogance. She learned how to play the piano without mastering it. She was invited to many society parties. She didn't know anything about books save what she had heard from people talking about them. Her primary concerns were methods of styling her hair, evening dresses, earrings, perfumes and shoes. Surely she had some admirers, though she didn't love any of them. Or so she claimed.

Yet I suspected she hadn't revealed to me the whole truth. So I conjured up a picture of her as a sixteen- or seventeen-year-old girl nurturing poetic visions in the depths of her heart, deriving passion and pleasure from them. For she said that no sooner had she turned eighteen than a manifest change befell her: she realized that her parents had become wealthy through a store that had started small and ended up as one of the largest businesses in the city, with many branches. They began imitating the landowning elite in their way of life. She determined to free herself, in her imagination at least, from the captivity of that kind of life, with all its haughtiness and affectation. She was annoyed with the studied organization of their large garden, which encircled their superfluously large house – seeing as it was only inhabited by the three of them and their two servants. She loved trees whose branches intertwined, trees that would burst from the ground with latent power, and she would frequent the forest, and wish that she could draw, for then she would draw those mighty, twisting tree trunks. Then she considered her body a tree that could feel the sap rushing through its parts. Her body blossomed, and she took pride in its blooms in silence. I told her, 'That was the buds' first flowering…' When her body reached maturity, she was tall, slender and beautiful, just as she wished to be. When she and I met, love conveyed a solar warmth to her body and her mind and ripened a new beauty within her: 'Here it is now, bearing fruit!' she said, throwing herself between my arms.

Suleiman Shanoub and his wife hadn't read a single book in all their busy lives. They hadn't heard of me until Sumaya told them about me. Her mother, who took pride in her daughter of such evident beauty and graceful physique, dreamed of a prince for her husband, not of a man whose name no one of consequence in the city had heard of. But Sumaya and I had fixed our intentions upon marriage. We were married in my two-room apartment, the address of which her parents didn't even know. Months passed, and it was as if the two of them were no longer counted among the living, while we thought ourselves the happiest two creatures on earth. The city, with all its possibilities for happiness, came upon us in one fell swoop. A number of literati, painters and professors rallied around us, and we were excessive in our mutual, though unfounded, admiration. We attracted the interest of an army of journalists, society ladies, scandalmongers, and art lovers. Sumaya stood in the midst of them, the very image of fortified beauty, or so I thought, whom eyes could see but hands couldn't touch. How astonished we were when her parents came to visit us one evening. In the morning, they sent us a piano, which occupied a large area in our small living room, and a letter addressed to 'Our two beloved children.' Two days later, they came to us again to transfer one of the houses they owned to Sumaya's name so that its annuity would accrue to us.

So if a man like Rashid attacked the desperate youth, discontent with life and the world, I would have added my voice to his. If in the city there were, as the winds of artistic progress pushed us forward, possibilities for growth, development and activity, just as there were possibilities for decay and death, wasn't it foolish of us to see only the barren and the ugly? I'd begun to see a new beauty, to relish a new pleasure, the likes of which I hadn't experienced before in the city. How fast I found myself part of a new social class! And what could be easier than forgetting that poverty exists? Yet I ignored the fact that I didn't know anything about Sumaya save a few delightful delusions I had bestowed upon her. I was incapable of shattering those delusions to fully grasp the greed in her heart.

All these thoughts flashed through my mind when I heard Rashid's words. At that very moment, Omar began defending his discontent and scorn.

'I'd like to take you by the hand, Rashid, and lead you, like Virgil led Dante, through the Hell of the Old City, and show you layer upon layer of people writhing from disease, children competing with dogs for a bone in the trash, and women crying out to God from the hunger gnawing at their insides. There you'll see one man knife another for the sake of a penny, and women sinking their fingernails into each other's faces for a few coins won by a pallid, emaciated child of theirs. Then perhaps you'd faint and fall to the ground like a rigid corpse…'

'Your eloquence won't affect me,' Rashid answered, 'and neither will your histrionic exaggerations. Bring me statistics, and I'll know how to treat the issue. What's the use of your sermonizing tone when you know that it only serves to change and distort the facts at your disposal? I've seen the Old City, and I admit that it's in a frightening state. But you – you take pleasure in knowing the state that it's in because it transports you to heights of verbal rapture. And that's worse than all the city's ugliness and shame. Tell us, Amin,' and he turned towards me, 'in the poor quarters, didn't you see enough smiling faces to exceed their likes anywhere else? Does poverty poison people's minds to the extent that Omar imagines?'

'That depends on two things,' I responded. 'Whether you see poverty from the inside or outside. When I was a little boy living with my mother and three siblings in a cramped, square room with a small paneless window, I don't think we complained too much. Our neighbors weren't any better off than we were, and our relatives weren't living in houses that were any better than ours, so there was no cause for envy. We were content with our lot. I remember how I used to read about famous men who *suffered poverty* in their youth, and I used to imagine that they lived like we did. Of course, I learned later that biographies of great men, when they speak of the 'poverty' of their hero, mean rather that he could afford no more than two servants and that his house was composed of only six rooms. At any rate, none of us consciously felt the wretchedness of his situation and the rottenness of the air he breathed. What everybody *did* fear was unemployment. As long as they had work to live on, it didn't matter to them if they ate a lot of meat or a little, or that they hadn't known, for example, the taste of chicken in their lives. On the contrary, the idea of eating chicken was a matter of joking and fun – chicken was 'for the rich folk,' and the imitation of 'the rich folk' in anything was cause for laughter. As for fighting, it was one of our deepest-rooted traditions. We'd quarrel and fight with extraordinary zeal, and then make up, and harmony would be restored between us with a lot of love and grace. But sometimes, the fighting could turn into an ongoing feud. It could recur at regular intervals, and lead to bitter arguments and court cases. It could even lead to murder. But when one lives in an environment such as that, one takes the ugliness and the need for granted. Because the quarter was so crowded, the contradictions in the quarter gave expression to all the contradictory emotions humanity contains. While three or four of the residents went about trading insults, others would sit on their doorsteps and sing. Suddenly you'd hear the sound of crying from the neighboring room and know who it was. There was no privacy there, but there was no one asking for it, either. Everybody knew everything about everybody else, and everyone was content with what he saw, even if he criticized, gloated, cursed or got angry. The whole community had cast an enclosure around itself, and in that enclosure, all felt they were a unit, however independent the parts within that dense unit were.'

Fares said jokingly, 'That's why poor people don't screw in the daytime; everyone can see what they're up to.'

'They've gotten so used to misery that they've come to love it,' Omar said. 'And that's the greatest cause for sorrow. There's no harm in loving squalor and filth if you're clean. But if you're squalid and filthy and love it – that's inexcusable.'

I resumed talking. 'But I only came to understand the reality of that situation years later, once I left the quarter to live by myself, far away from it, and it was possible for me to see it from the outside.

'One November evening I came across an old friend of mine, a neighbor of ours from the Old City. We were about the same age and had spent many long hours in our younger days talking about our hopes and dreams, trading secrets about our trivial romances or comments about the neighborhood folk, the young and the old. I hadn't seen him for six or seven years. Even if he hadn't changed much during that time, I could sense in spite of myself that a fissure had grown between us as I noted his yellowed teeth, his soiled clothes, his many curses, and his crude behavior. When he began reminding me of bygone days, I simply melted from the longing, despite my internal resistance. He reminded me how I used to write love letters for him that the post would swallow up with no response, how we did this and how we did that. So I said to him, 'Let's go to a restaurant for dinner together and reminisce about some of those dear memories.' At the restaurant, he informed me he still worked as a blacksmith in a small workshop and was married and had three children and all the rest. He still lived in the same old room. By the time we finished dinner, my friend had drunk a good deal of cognac and burst forth in a boisterous mirth, talking without interruption. When we left the restaurant, a light rain was falling. He insisted I accompany him to his house and yelled, 'What, are you too good for us, Amin?' I suggested we take a taxi, and he laughed derisively and said, 'Like the rich folk? No, Amin. Walk on your own two feet, like me.' So we walked. When we reached the Old City, the rain was pouring so violently that we had to stop in doorways every now and then for shelter. Then he said that he knew a place nearby we could wait until the rain stopped. He took me to a dive with a low ceiling whose patrons were drinking arak or playing cards in a great clamor. I almost tripped when I saw them all turn towards me, a newcomer there, their glances flashing with contempt like the glint of a knife's edge. I didn't know how to behave or how to speak in order to make myself acceptable to them. My friend still spoke freely, cursing with passion and showing me off to his friends.

'It was almost midnight, so I said I had to go home because my wife didn't know where I was. But he refused to accept that as an excuse. He grabbed my arm violently and shoved me down the poorly lit alleyways. The alleyways twisted and turned more than I remembered, and the houses leaned close enough to embrace each other above my head. The rain didn't stop, and the water began running in streams alongside the walls or in the middle of our path until we reached an area that resembled a deep trench lined with houses of every size and color. Our clothes had gotten so wet that the moisture had almost reached our bodies. The path wasn't paved, and when we weren't stepping in the gurgling stream, we were stumbling in the sticky mud. No sooner did we see the houses of the quarter in the depths of the trench than my friend tugged me by the arm. His throat emitted a soft cry, short and sharp. The water had gathered at the bottom of the ditch and formed a large pond that shone with a terrifying brightness. The houses' upper floors stood out above the flood, and we ran down towards them. Terror gripped my throat. Garbage had accumulated in the faulty sewers, clogging them and rendering them useless. The streams gushing from the nearby streets had joined into one torrential current, poured into the lower quarter, and settled there. The room in which I had spent almost ten years of my childhood was half-submerged, and two drowned boys were dragged from the putrid yellow water while their mother wailed and cried. There was not one house which the waters didn't cover to the height of at least one meter, and pieces of old furniture floated in and out of box-like rooms. The residents stumbled in the water, carrying their precious belongings to store them with their neighbors living on the upper floors. Men and women began bailing the water in buckets and pitchers and dumping it in a small patch of land surrounded by a high wall, which the quarter's residents had hoped to turn into a garden one day. The young women rolled their pants up past their knees to work alongside the men. People from neighboring houses came rushing to the rescue, and I soon found myself carrying water with everyone else, lifting children above the flood to take them to a safe place, and pushing cupboards and cabinets to the dry areas. I got separated from my friend during the mêlée. When I saw him again, after the sky had exhausted its anger, he told me that his wife and children had escaped the danger. But we had to keep toiling until the dawn's early hours. When some of us finally managed to clear the drains, the water retreated into them. Garbage from the roads, which the streams had swept into the quarter, mixed with the filth from the smaller sewage pipes, which had burst from the sewage inside them. All of it was left behind in the houses.

'The quarter folk probably forgot the flood in a few weeks. But I'll never forget it.'

I gulped down the dregs of my beer, got up immediately, and said, 'Pardon me! Time flew by, and I missed an appointment. I have to go, and fast…'

Then I left.

I returned to the long, winding road. I'd almost forgotten my appointment with Inayat Yasser, so I quickened my pace.

The memory of the flood aroused in my mind the memory of the other event, connected to the flood, that happened that same night.

The night gave way to a grave morning, when the quarter folk began dispersing, all of them pale-faced and haggard, enervated, shaking from the cold. I too was shaking and sneezing in my soaked clothes. Some of them made us tea. I drank three or four cups just to be able to stand. Not one resident from the lower floors was spared harm, and several children had drowned. When there was nothing left for me to do, I took my leave and headed home, dragging my feet.

I entered my house silently so as not to disturb Sumaya. When I went into the bedroom, I found her bed empty and untouched. I vaguely realized that she wasn't there. But I didn't think about it too much, because I took my clothes off, lay down on the bed, and sank into a deep sleep.

Chapter Five

Sumaya wasn't there. She'd abandoned me. She'd abandoned me, leaving only a blue sheet of her letter paper, on which she'd written three lines begging me not to worry about her because she'd left me of her own accord. Worry about her! The world had collapsed in ruins around me by the time I contacted her parents. They didn't know anything about what she'd done, and it occurred to me that a nefarious connection existed between the events of the day before: my friend as he conjured up my past, the pouring rain in the Old City, the flood, the drowned children in my old home – then Sumaya's disappearance, for which I found no justification.

My mind was ajumble. It appeared to me that my life had suddenly exploded, and fragments of it had been hurled against one another in the air only to fall and bury me under the ruin and rubble. Happiness then appeared like glass broken and glinting throughout my shattered imagination, where people too were scattered like fragments of furniture. Nothing true or meaningful survived apart from two things: the flood and Sumaya's disappearance. I began thinking of the state of the city in wide symbols and allusions that reflected my defeat and disappointment, and my heart bled in sadness for the thousands of people who carried the weight of the city upon their lean bodies, who fed it with their flesh and blood, who filled the land with small joys and copious tears. In that moment I contemplated love's crushed corpse as decay seeped into it, marking my life with a stain from which I would find no deliverance.

Sumaya had left behind most of her clothes, and the closet still overflowed with her dresses, blouses, skirts and shoes. She must have taken only the suitcase she'd bought several weeks before, claiming we might need it if we went on a trip to the mountain. Her flight, then, was not a surprise whim, but a planned affair. When I began searching for details, searching for friends and male acquaintances in order to find out who her lover was – would she have abandoned me if not for a lover she had concealed from me? – I only found one thing: she'd fled with eight thousand pounds. She'd sold the house her parents had given her, from which we'd profited by renting out. Without my knowledge she had sold it for eight thousand pounds – less than its true value – and left the city.

Whenever I tried to discover the mystery behind her flight,

I resembled a man running up against a wall that had neither cracks nor openings. I began reviewing our past together but could only remember those burning hours I'd spent with her in bed as she vacillated between laughter and tears, between violence and submissiveness. I began to ask, What did she do in the morning or the evening, when I was away from home, at work editing the newspaper? We had a female cook who took care of the house under Sumaya's supervision, but... The cook didn't know anything, or else I would have heard it from her after my wife's disappearance. Whenever Sumaya was gone during the first part of the night, I knew she was at her mother's, or that they were together visiting friends. Besides all that, there only remained that anxious love I showered her with. I searched our bedroom for traces and clues with which to seek even part of the truth, but I could only find my little gifts to her, and my own papers, most of which contained descriptions of her beauty. But I also understood the reason she'd fired the cook three days before her disappearance.

The only thing to do was accept the blow and adjust my life to my new circumstances. But I couldn't. Whenever I was exasperated and mad with fury at Sumaya, I only became less capable of diverting my mind from her. She would come to me naked night after night, while I was alone in the small house and unable to sleep. I killed her one thousand and one times in my dreams, but just as many times did I cover her with my kisses.

I got out of bed one day and admitted to myself that I was truly insane. Otherwise, how could I let myself disintegrate and corrode from a woman's betrayal? How dare I see the threads of the misery of thousands of the city's inhabitants interwoven with my own defeat in love? Had I begun to think, unconsciously, that what drove Sumaya to betray me was her money? What about her leisure time? And my stupidity in not seeing the truth of it?

I stopped working at the newspaper for a long time. I began sleeping in, walking the streets till lunchtime, sleeping for most of the afternoon, and in the evening, descending to the streets again, carrying a mind in which gloomy fantasies propagated ceaselessly. I was sick, sick to death: I would ruminate on the roots of the heavens, trample the bones of the dead and see the hungry masses, their canines bared, preying upon their victims. I felt death embracing the land and sea, filling the air with the stench of disintegrating corpses, watering the parched trees with the blood of the youth, youth and decay, love and the decay of love. Love feeds death, and sex is a symbol of death. Death without comfort. And God laughs throughout the night, throughout the day, throughout eternity.

Chapter Six

I passed by the cinema as it expelled a multicolored throng from dazzlingly lit galleries and cast them into caverns of darkness. Everything in the cinema's darkness had proceeded according to the watchers' desires. The differences between them had disappeared, and their eyes were glued to a vision of themselves playing the roles of the lovers and adventurers. But as soon as the lights came on and the exit music began to play, people saw each other's faces again, and the sweet delusion disappeared. They realized they had to return in flocks and herds to actual places, few of which lived up to their desires, and where the struggle seldom ended in a embraces and kisses.

When I began to make my way between the flowing crowd, I felt my total isolation from humanity. Yet those were the people whose lives I'd contemplated, whose futures I'd pitied while fear and worry lay latent in their eyes. I had sat month after month, like a prophet burdened by the years, thinking about their maladies. No doubt I only saw my own misery in the misery of humanity – that's why I kept staring at them. For in the death of love I had tasted the bitterness of the death of hope. And I saw throngs of humanity pushing each other right and left while despair hovered over them all.

I recalled how Omar al-Sameri got upset with me one day. He began telling me in a tone mixed with affection and anger, 'You had the chance to free yourself from the fetters of love, but instead, you sat down among the dead to examine the corpses. You're rejecting the sparkle in women's eyes so that you can clutch at skulls with empty eye sockets, when in reality you've only played a mind trick on yourself by making love and death one thing. You will remain stuck in the mire, Amin. And you won't be able to challenge the will of life and subject it to your own by dragging about the misfortune of humanity. That's just a mind trick; you won't reach any spiritual contentment through it. You've isolated yourself from the course of reality. And this isolation of yours isn't the isolation of the ascetic enraptured in his prayers but the isolation of a rake battling a conscience that urges him to feel regret. You regret your love as if it were a crime you committed and you were no longer capable of deliverance from its consequences. And that's ridiculous of you – you'll find that after a while, your mind will turn into something more like a remote, isolated castle that no one even cares to attack, until it falls apart and collapses of its own accord. No benefit's to be expected from that, Amin. The city needs sound and dynamic minds that create and invent, to do in our lives the work of the sun and the wind. Don't think for a second that I don't like women, or that I don't grieve for the misery of the poor, but I assure you: I won't let anything in existence distort for me the image of life and truth…'

It was then that I began writing my third successful book, after a creative drought that had lasted three years. The book caught the attention of the Yasser family – Inayat and Roxane – one of the city's oldest and richest. After Inayat Hanem summoned me, she informed me that she and her sister admired my ability to conjure up the past and depict those who had died long ago to fill the pages of my books, as well as my familiarity with the life of the popular masses, out of which I made a framework that enclosed my books' principal themes, and my – and here I quote! – 'terrifying and pleasing' way of casting my books' characters into an environment of uncommon carnality and violent pain. For that reason, she and her sister had decided on asking me to collaborate with them to write a history of the Yasser family, for they supposed that such a book would fill a gap in the history of the city and serve every citizen who'd studied its developments during the last three hundred years.

I wasn't very enthusiastic about it. Why should I burden myself with the responsibility of resurrecting a bunch of aristocrats? Wouldn't it be better for them to remain in their obscure graves for all eternity? But Inayat Hanem was as obstinate as any woman of fifty-five years or so. She pointed out that her paternal grandfather was the founder of the city's college, that one of her paternal uncles was the greatest poet the city had ever known (I didn't agree with her, of course, especially because all his poetry was in Turkish), that her grandfather had left behind many pieces of sheet music, and that his life was full of the intrigues of both power and love (later we discovered papers that alluded to his rape of one of his virgin female relatives). In addition to that, the family had spawned a number of illustrious women, including an author (no one today has heard of her) whose manuscripts, had they not been preserved in an iron box, would have been eaten by rats; a ravishing beauty endowed with a *wonderful personality* who caused a number of scandals in the region and was later forced to travel to Europe, where she passed away; and so on and so forth.

I finally accepted Inayat Hanem's proposal. Our agreement was that she would pay me a monthly salary and that I would work with her in the evenings, between eight o'clock and midnight. That way, the day would be at my disposal. The one condition was that we finish the book in two years. I told myself that such a job would occupy me and teach me the necessity of mental disengagement and objective thinking, during which time I could write a book about Sumaya. Once I emptied my veins of the last dregs of love, I would leave the city and move abroad.

When I saw the cinema crowd pouring forth to fill the street, I remembered a chapter I'd written about the public immolation of Ghazi Pasha Yasser, one of Inayat Hanem's ancestors. That incident was the turning point in their family history, the point that marked the beginning of their decline from a mighty ruling family to a mere wealthy family trying desperately to revive its former glory. Ghazi Pasha starred in a scene that has now become another banal event in local history for the frequency of its repetition: For many years, Ghazi had been beloved of the people, and everyone considered him their protector against the caprices of the Ottoman sultanate. But one day he suddenly fell in their eyes, and the masses banded together against him from every corner. They seized him outside his castle as he sat astride his horse, pulled him down between their feet, dragged him in the dirt, and hung him on a post. After that, they lowered him into a blazing fire. His limbs flailed about in the flames, sending his fat to spatter the spectators while they yelled and danced around him.

I knew the masses were incapable of suppressing the savagery latent in their folds, ever ready to show its teeth and claws. Whenever I had to pass through different classes of people, I feared that they would touch me, even if unintentionally, and infect me with their terrible disease. Yet not a long time had passed since I'd delighted in walking among crowds of people, just to sense their bodily presence. I didn't blame myself – or commend myself either – for my mercurial emotions. Perhaps there was nothing to the matter save my own self! All the love and hate I had showered upon myself – when I tried to regain my balance, I then projected that love and hate upon the masses, which I had made into a reflection of myself.

As the crowds leaving the cinema dispersed and people started walking about me in pairs and alone, serenity returned to me. After I remembered the story of Ghazi Pasha, I imagined Inayat and Roxane lurking in their library before a new pile of letters and manuscripts, and wondered: What kinds of echoes reverberated in the minds of those two spinsters along with the voices of their ancestors, strident and bursting with the vigor of muscle and sensation? Giving free rein to their frantic imaginations, Inayat and her sister sat comfortably amidst whole generations of rabble. Yet they couldn't endure proximity to the common folk in their own era. Inayat despised movie theaters and called them 'the symbol of the utmost vulgarity' and Roxane, Inayat's half-sister by their father and her junior by fifteen years or more, refused to walk in the street for more than five minutes. Her car was an absolute necessity to distance herself from the commoners.

Each of the two sisters was crazy in her own right. Inayat Hanem kept the present at arm's length in order to live in the clamor of the past. And Roxane had inherited from her ancestors their vigorous blood and lusty passions. She had a certain beauty to her, and when she stood opposite her skinny elderly sister, her spirit's passion for the pleasures of the body would appear in the way she tilted and swayed. She had a number of lovers despite her strange aristocratic traits. If she did get swept away by passion for a short while, she wouldn't know how to fix her love in one spot, and she would wander elsewhere with it. She wasn't married and didn't care to be. I'd heard stories that, perhaps hypocritically, pointed to violent sexual tendencies of hers, which didn't escape my notice. Maybe that was what made her such good company.

Her sister Inayat, the virgin spinster, couldn't stand Roxane's romances at first. She eventually got used to them and accepted them without comment. Every now and then, Roxane would fill the Yasser family palace with the din and tumult of one of her famous parties where, most often, male singers and nearly naked female dancers entertained the guests. Or Roxane would take an oud (from a number of musical instruments her grandfather had left behind), play it, and sing Turkish songs. Inayat would get upset by Roxane's voice and descend to the basement, if it were summertime, where the spoils of the past had piled up. Or she would go up to her bedroom and busy herself with the family's manuscripts, most of which had rotted and decayed. I discovered that, in hours such as these, she would take a bottle of cognac to cheer her in her solitude.

Chapter Seven

'Amin! Amin!'

I heard a voice calling me. It was Nasser al-Hamawi running after me with some books under his arm. 'Good evening, Nasser,' I said.

'I've been looking for you everywhere.'

'Why?'

As if whispering a secret, he said, 'I want your help. I've written a long piece, a short book, really, about the development of the societal life of the city during the last century.'

'Wonderful! Have you given up poetry?'

'How could I give up poetry, Amin? It's just that, in the last few months, I've worked on this book as a kind of mental exercise. I want your help publishing it.'

'I think I prefer your poetry to your prose. But I'll see what I can do.'

Nasser laughed and said, 'It's strange – my poetry has also become social lately.'

'That's unfortunate, after those wonderful poems in rajaz meter that you published.'

'Now I write elegies. I've written five. The first one's title is 'Elegy for the Death of a Store Owner.''

'A store owner?'

'Yes. The second one is about the death of a chauffeur.'

'Are you serious, Nasser?'

'Of course. The five elegies treat the five aspects of death which residents of all cities in the world are familiar with. Have you noticed that cities are built upon man's fear of death? It seems to me that man contemplates death in order to be conscious of life. But how does this simple theory affect the life of a store owner or a laborer or a beggar?'

'It doesn't affect their lives. All there is to it is this: an instinctual drive to survive urges them on, nothing more and nothing less.'

He laughed again and said, 'Simple as that, then, huh? Anyway, I'm sorry, I have to go, and in the opposite direction. When can you see me about the book?'

'Come over the day after tomorrow, in the morning. But remember, Nasser, I still prefer your poetry! Goodbye.'

The five aspects of death! As if I hadn't stuffed my soul fit to bursting with thoughts of death in the last two years. Ah, I really am fed up, and I have to find a way out…and the road is long and never-ending, and the lofty buildings loom like a woman squatting with all her weight upon my shoulders, the buildings' arches like open wounds in the darkness, while stars adorn the black sky above. And my friend Nasser comes to tell me about the five aspects of death! Suddenly I felt a clamor of voices surging within me, raising me, and casting me into the days of my childhood in the village. In the village I didn't think about death at all. I didn't think it was possible for me to die or for any of my near and dear to die either. Whenever I saw a man shrouded on his deathbed and regarded the glassy pallor that had descended on his face and hands, whenever a tremor of fear of an unknown nature invaded my insides, I thought something like that could only happen to those outside the bounds of my love, and that whatever my love embraced would remain forever alive, whole, beautiful. I used to walk in funeral processions where I would see women wailing and tearing at their braids, and men weeping silently. I'd listen closely to the hymns of the worshippers as they humbled themselves before God, and in their prayers repeated the words 'the gardens of eternity.' The funeral procession would descend into narrow streets overlooking a wide green valley, where from afar I would sometimes hear a shepherd playing a flute. The words 'gardens of eternity' would wind themselves around my mind, and propel my imagination from the world of sadness and despair to valleys with bottomless depths and twisting paths, where shepherds live with their flocks and the melodies of their flutes. In the cemetery, the white-bearded priest would pray behind clouds of incense. People would take handfuls of dirt and throw them into the grave, and they would fall in successive thumps upon the wooden coffin. Then I would bend over to take a bit of dirt between my fingers and cast it upon the dead man, thereby appeasing both God and my conscience. The women would wail and cry, and some of the men would erupt in groans like the bellow of a stabbed bull, and tears would pour forth upon their cheeks. My stomach would sink, my lungs would contract, and my throat would emit a soft cry that sent tears to my eyes, tears I couldn't hold back. But as soon as I returned to the road overlooking the valley, all sadness would vanish from my mind. The valley could be devoid of flowers, with nothing in it save green ears of wheat. Yet I imagined only gardens bursting with flowers, all of them beaming with color. The pallor of death would be transformed into the yellow of a pretty flower, an emblem of vigor and life. The nameless yellow flowers would jostle together in my imagination, and I would see them undulating in a spring wind, then inclining above me as I myself lay among them and surrendered to sleep.

On days when I didn't see the trace of a tree or flower in the city's neighborhoods, those imaginary flowers kept me company. I would go to school, devour every book that fell into my hands, and nourish in secret my small dream of the flowers lest the old walls collapsing around me finished it off.

Long, slow years passed before I triumphed in my mental battle against that lean, barren life with no plants or flowers, and against death, continuous in its harvest of the people of the alleys, which no longer aroused in my mind images of the flowers of gardens. Then Sumaya appeared, wearing yellow blouses and green skirts in different shades, as if my imaginary flower had become incarnate in the form of a woman.

One morning, shortly after we first met, we set out before sunrise. (How many feminine wiles did she resort to with her parents so that she could go out at such early hours!) We rode bicycles to the forest, where we began singing loudly, running down the paths and climbing the trees. I filled her hair with red anemones, and then we headed towards the bridge. We would stop every minute or two to steal a kiss. Her lips were hot, but her cheeks, arms and shins were as cold as marble. On the ancient, dilapidated bridge – an old ruin with a piece of rock upon it engraved with the name of a ruler described as 'King of Kings, Sultan of Sultans, Ruler of Land and Sea' – we stopped and looked around. The sun had risen, and in that calm green world that reverberated only with our cries, we were the only ones there. We rolled up our pant legs, jumped in the sparkling brook, and our bare feet struck the soft pebbles on the creek bed, tickling us and making us laugh. Sumaya had smooth, shiny calves, uncommonly well made, but she blushed with shyness whenever I commented on them after that.

'What sculptor fashioned those calves?' I asked.

She laughed and said, 'Your imagination!'

'You look like a Greek statue,' I said. 'Maybe you're not made of marble but of flower petals.'

'No,' she said, 'I'm made of flesh and blood,' and she pelted me with handfuls of anemones overflowing from her bicycle basket.

I still imagined her as a yellow flower, though wilting and wan. How I wished for someone from the crowds of people to come and tell me, 'I saw Sumaya a few moments ago. She's dead.' Then I would have telephoned Inayat Hanem to apologize for not going to her place that evening. I would have gone to a small, quiet cafe to recompose, with my reflections, the beautiful past. But something like that would never happen. When I approached the Great Square, the heart of the city, I saw black shapes of men standing in doorways, expelled by the stream of humanity. They leaned on walls with cigarettes dangling from their mouths, their hands planted deep in their pockets. 'What are they thinking about?' I wondered. 'Their loved ones? Their enemies? Or the futility of their hours, devoid of love?' Any one of them could have emerged to ask me, 'Would you like to stand with me in this dark corner and listen to my story? Ah, but I see that you're dead. What's that strange yellow flower in your hand?' Instead of that, a woman with bulging eyes and rouged lips approached, reached out her hand to stop me, and whispered, 'Do you want a nice young lady tonight?'

Chapter Eight

When I could walk no more, I hailed a taxi. It took me past the streetlights fast falling behind us and sped me on to the road up the mountain. After a few minutes, its headlights sent forth a ray of light that swept between the trees lining both sides of the road, their boughs meeting in towering arches above us. It finally alighted before on the steps of the Yasser family palace.

As soon as she opened the door, the servant girl Safiya said, in that drowsy way of hers, 'Roxane Hanem is waiting for you in the library.'

In the library I saw Roxane wearing a black robe and standing near piles of papers with an old yellow book in her hand. It looked like she'd been reading from it. I immediately realized that those pages were the manuscripts I'd spent the last months poring over and studying. I was astonished to see Roxane like that – beforehand, she hadn't shown such great interest in our work that she would arrive before her sister to sift through the decayed papers with which the palace's basement brimmed. I'd hardly said 'Good evening' when she replied, 'Good evening, Mr. Amin. I tried to get in touch with you a number of times, but no one knew where you were on the mountain. So perhaps you don't know that my sister Inayat died six days ago.'

I stopped in my tracks. I didn't know what to say for a few moments. 'She died?'

'No doubt she would have wanted you to walk in her funeral procession. She was very fond of you.'

'God rest her soul.'

'Now there's no one in this enormous house except for me. And it terrifies me to recall that I'm the last surviving member of my family. Since her death, I've infringed on my sister's rights by searching through her papers, hoping to find her place and mine in our long genealogy. Who was the founder of the family?'

'Tajeddine Yasser, one of Saladin's commanders in the Crusades.'

'That's right. Tajeddine Yasser. Surely you've read most of these papers?'

Her voice was inflected with ridicule, which puzzled me. I answered her, saying, 'Perhaps you know, Roxane Hanem, that I read them with great care alongside Inayat Hanem.'

'Yes, I know that,' she replied, the bitterness increasing in her voice. 'My sister loved the history of her family. I've never known someone like her, to sacrifice herself and efface her personality for the sake of her ancestors' glory. Ever since I learned of my older sister's existence as a child, more than thirty years ago, I can't remember her thinking of anything else except the Yasser family: the Yasser family and the Fatimids, the Yasser family and the Ottomans, the Yasser family and Napoleon, the Yasser family and Muhammad Ali Pasha, the Yasser family here, the Yasser family there. She loved nothing save the secrets of their lives and their disgusting clothes that filled the house.'

'But is it really so unusual for someone to be concerned with the history of their ancestors?'

'Inayat spent her life wallowing in the mud of the past. She offered her youth, her mind, her body, as a sacrifice on the altar of the family – this family of which no trace remains except me. She made her lone task in life the study of our conditions and circumstances since the beginning of creation, following the greatness of this man and the fall of that, this one's travels and that one's romances, so that she could arrange it all into one large history book. Yet with her work, she only filled the house with the stench of corpses and the clatter of bones. She became so enraptured with her oh-so-necessary work that she herself shrank – unknowingly – into a bag of bones. And now she's gone and died, and the book is still in its beginning stages. But she left a clause in her will that'll interest you. She says you're to be given two thousand pounds if you finish what you started on the history of the Yasser family in 150,000 words.'

She stopped talking. As for me, I was trying to come to grips with the new situation. 'That was kind of her,' I said. 'And I would be delighted to continue writing the book. But it seems you're not content with that.'

'No, I'm not content, Amin. I'm not content at all. In the past, thinking about this project only used to bother me. But now I despise it, and reject it. And don't think I don't know the reasons you might try to defend it: the importance of history, the elaboration of events, mental enlightenment, national pride, cultural values, and other such things. Starting today, none of that concerns me anymore. My mind was infected by Inayat, and like her, I allowed myself to fall into a pit of the past, a pit that devoured me. But I fought and struggled, and fought and struggled, until I felt, at the hour of her death, that the pit was spitting me out, to return to the present, to life, to life.'

'But what's the problem if *I* devote myself to writing your family history with the passion and care of an artist? It's your right to live however you want, to free yourself from the power of your ancestors.'

'How can I free myself from their power when these letters, memoirs and manuscripts lie strewn across my path for me to trip over for the rest of my life? And when you finish your book, I'll be the only person who'll have to bear the burden of it – won't I?'

'Then what do you suggest?'

She looked into my eyes and responded with a sure and intent voice, 'I propose to destroy the past.'

'Destroy the past?'

That expression sounded insane to me.

She was silent for a moment. Then she resumed her speech, her voice rining with an unexpected tone of entreaty. 'Try to appreciate my position on this, Amin. This enormous palace, all of it, is mine – and I don't want it. I have a few thousand acres in the neighboring villages – and I don't want them. I have all these papers and scaps here and in the basement rooms – and I don't want them. They're nothing but the appendages of the past and the tools to embellish it, the garments of death that Inayat sacrificed her life for...'

She stopped for a moment and added, 'But what I want now is the present. I want a present alive and free. Don't you think I've gotten old, Amin? What you see on my face is nothing but the shadows of old age cast by these ancient, crumbling walls.'

I hadn't expected such words from Roxane, known as she was for her reckless outbursts in the pursuit of pleasure. 'I don't think the shadows of old age are capable of falling on you,' I said.

She approached me, looked into my eyes, and with a smile of surrender on her painted lips, said, 'You haven't lived between these walls, so you wouldn't understand. You wouldn't understand…' She looked as if she were faltering, as if she were having trouble saying what she wanted to. Suddenly she headed for the window and called out angrily, 'I want to be delivered from all that surrounds me. My soul contains a lust for life that would be enough for ten women. Amin,' she said, turning towards me, 'What do you think of me?'

'You're a very attractive woman.'

'Are you trying to flatter me?'

'Why would I do that?'

In a low voice, she said, 'Will you marry me?'

Dear God! She surprised me. Her insanity must have carried her away. Yet I scrutinized her face in silence, and I looked at her as one looks at a woman he desires. Perhaps she was almost forty…and I almost thirty…but her cheeks were still tight and her lips weren't flabby. But to marry her…that was another matter. How could I, in my romanticism, imagine a marriage not built on love? Marrying her would only mean I coveted her money.

'But Roxane,' I said – and I pitied her, as if thanking her for her desire to marry me – 'you know that I'm married, legally.'

'I know that. But your wife abandoned you and hid from you for two whole years. You could easily get a divorce.'

How simple the matter was for Roxane! Two whole years had passed me by as I embraced Sumaya's ghost. I hadn't thought about divorce for a second. My tongue was tied, and I didn't say a word.

Roxane turned to a stack of old papers, took some of them in her hand and examined them in silence, one by one.

I could hear soft gusts of wind on the trees, and listened intently. Suddenly the wind bore me the image of Sumaya dancing against the wind in a flowing blue dress whose hem lifted to reveal two long, marmoreal legs. In Roxane's posture, however, I saw only the balancing act of the crow as she clutched the family papers to her taut, raised chest. Then she said, 'I'm going to burn all these papers. I'm going to burn them now.'

I was shaken from my dream and cried out to her, 'What? You're going to burn the papers we spent so much energy on?'

'These papers are my property, and I'll administer my property however I want. If you marry me, you won't find this burden waiting for you to bear wherever you go. I'll sell this house and all my estates, and I'll build a modern house in another part of the city. Then you'll be able to write, free and unfettered from the chains of poverty and need. Did I say that I would sell this house? No. I'll get rid of it. I'll destroy it. I'll destroy it.'

She walked towards the wall, pressed an electric button, and said, 'I don't need an answer from you now, Amin. Go home and think about it. You'll be free of worry, and I'll be free of my dusty bygone glory. And we'll have nothing but the flame of the present…'

The servant entered, and Roxane said, 'Safiya, bring me a bottle of kerosene. I have some papers here that I want to burn in the fireplace.' The servant left.

'You're crazy, Roxane!' I shouted. 'You have no right to deprive me of two thousand pounds!'

She didn't turn back towards me. Instead, she bent down, lifted a large quantity of papers in her hands, and stuffed them in the fireplace, saying, 'This is a treasure that Inayat bequeathed me…Oh! I have to burn them in groups…and when we marry, you'll discover other treasures.'

'But suppose we don't get married.'

'Then you'll have to write the book from memory. I hereby allow you to make it all up, from beginning to end!'

The servant returned with a flask of kerosene, and Roxane ordered her to pour a little of it onto the pile in the fireplace. Soon a beautiful fire broke out, moaning and extending its flaming tongues towards the chimney's flue. Roxane picked up another pile of scraps and, in the light of the flames, began to read lines here and there and intersperse between the phrases her short, piercing bursts of laughter.

"*And when everyone was seated, all of them burning with passion for what I'd promised them, the door opened wide and Loubab entered in a wrap made of gold, a tambourine in her hand and veiled dancing women behind her…*" Into the fire! "*She beseeched me, and said 'Cover my shame lest I throw myself in the river.' So I said to her,*

'*Shall I show you the most direct route to the river?*' Who was that? I wonder. "*Orda, Ahmet Ağa oturmuş, ağzındaki gülü ile tatlı musiki dinleyerek ısınyordu…and there Ahmad Agha sat, with a rose in his mouth, as lethargy caressed him to the sound of sweet music. The day was oppressively hot, so one of them said, 'Why don't we lie down here and sleep?' And I recalled the lines of an old poet who surrendered to sleep on the streambank one fragrant April day and dreamed a wondrous dream…*" She laughed hysterically and said, 'How beautiful this language is! Into the fire!'

I gazed on her as she reveled in burning those papers, and didn't know what curse to hurl in her face. I had become very fond of some of those old scraps after having pored over them with no particular desire. Since I was merely hired to study them, I suppose I could have watched the fire devour them without feeling pained. Yet I found Roxane's attempt to destroy her family's past with such boisterousness absolutely repugnant. If she had determined to deliver herself from a prison built by the remains of her ancestors, then I had nothing to criticize her for. But I was disgusted at her insistence on carrying out her will before me in such a manner, as if in doing so, she were forcing my assent. No doubt her wealth was tempting bait for any man, and Lord knows I needed some of her money. Was it not in her power to emphasize her wealth instead of destroying her past, so that I could linger for a while to consider her proposal? In the flames that were finishing off bundle after bundle of those manuscripts, I saw the same flames that had finished off her old ancestor before the eyes of the masses.

She lifted her eyes towards me and asked loudly, 'Why are you standing there not uttering a sound? You must be disgusted with me. But Amin, I have at most twenty more years to live, and I'll spend them how I so desire, not how those old scoundrels would have me do – they're nothing but dirt in their graves. Safiya!' She turned to her servant. 'Go to Inayat's bedroom, and you'll find a large black box full of papers. Bring them to me in bunches.'

Once Safiya had closed the door behind her, I approached Roxane and said, 'Why don't you stop burning the papers until I reach a decision regarding our marriage? If we really do marry, I'd ask you to give me these papers as a gift. And if not—'

'No, no, my dear. We must finish off the remains of the dead before everything else. If you marry me, I'll want to feel that I'm a new woman, or as the poets say, a phoenix rising from the ashes of her past.'

A gleam of desire flashed before my eyes, illuminating her beauty for a fleeting second. But the face of Sumaya, with her long flowing hair and wide amber eyes, appeared for a moment and transformed Roxane's face into a deformed blotch. So I turned my back to her and headed towards the door.

'Amin!' she cried out.

I turned to see her throwing a new group of papers into the fire. 'I'll ask you to inform me of your decision tomorrow,' she said. And I'll ask you to come in the early morning because I'll be waiting for you. Or call me. Tomorrow morning.'

Suddenly she stood up straight and drew near me. In her eyes was that sexual glint that hadn't stopped shining in the eyes of the Yasser family since epochs long past. When I extended my hand to shake hers in farewell, she took it. Then she raised her lips towards mine and kissed me.

Chapter Nine

When I heard the huge door close behind me, I felt as if I'd been released after a long prison sentence. The wind, the same wind I'd heard inside, blew in my face, cold and pure, carrying a rushing sound like laughter. When I descended to the long pathway surrounded by trees, I told myself I must find salvation in a release like that of the wind – those laughing forces of nature. But where could I find such a thing?

I was sad about Inayat Hanem's death, and wasn't pleased about giving up writing the Yasser family history. And just like that, two thousand pounds had turned to ashes and smoke right when I needed them. But I wasn't so concerned. And who knew? Perhaps Roxane was right about what she did.

In the starlight there appeared before me a statue of Aphrodite, the goddess of love, standing between the trees. A blue ray of light had fallen on the incline of her shoulder, and the light made one of her arms appear like a dry, twisting bough. I stood looking at her, even though I'd seen her many times before. No one quite knew the history of the statue, but a Yasser family forbear most probably brought it, around two hundred years before, from one of the Greek islands when they were under Turkish control. I struck a match with caution, and before the wind blew it out, I glimpsed the wounds of time upon Aphrodite's marmoreal body. What storms had lashed her, what rains cleansed her, and what suns kissed her in the centuries long past while she stood coquettishly covering her middle with a long-fingered hand? A plant had crept upon the statue's base and left a pile of dead leaves at her feet. When I turned to leave her, I was thinking about Roxane's request, and asked myself: Should I accept it and find myself a wealthy man with marble statues in my garden?

But I cast a last glance behind me and started in fear, for I saw the goddess of love move. In order to convince myself of the ridiculousness of that fancy, I turned towards the statue again and stared at it with intense resolution. It was still, eternally still. And I laughed at myself.

Chapter Ten

My return home this time was effortless, and I didn't feel exhaustion chewing away at my brain. A new yearning came over me, stirring my chest, and I felt a lightness in my body as if water were raising me up to float upon it with ease.

It was a lightness in my limbs and joints I had known in the days of my childhood in the village, and I imagined myself in the valley jumping from rock to rock between the olive trees, searching for the small pools between the rocks, and picking the little wildflowers that had settled within the cracks.

Once a friend and I surprised my father in the monastery garden. We asked him for some apples, and he told us he would give us all the apples we wanted if we would first help him dig the small channels he was preparing for irrigation. While we were sweating at our work, he began telling us story after story, one of which I remembered that night.

The story revolves around a man on his deathbed as he gives his son a final piece of advice. The man says, "If women ever dash your hopes, go to your friends, for friendship is deeper than love. And if all your friends desert you, fall back on your wealth, for wealth creates flatterers to amuse and relax you. But if you find that, from poor planning, you have squandered your money, if not a friend is left to you, and if the darkness of despair has descended upon your heart, then know that you were a failure in life and that it's best you put an end to it. For that reason, son, I've prepared you this ring, which you see hanging from the middle of the ceiling, to use in your suicide.'

'As our friend was an ignorant and inexperienced young man, fate knocked him down. The women he was fond of abandoned him, and the friends whom he loved did the same. He spent his very last penny, and realized that the only thing left for him to do was to get a rope and take it to the aforementioned ring to hang himself. He got up on a chair, tied the rope to the ring, put the noose around his neck, and jumped off the chair – and suddenly found himself upon the ground, the ceiling's plaster falling on him and gold coins pouring down like rain! Among the gold, he found a letter from his father that said, 'Son,

111

I knew that life would drag you down to these depths. That's why I arranged a new life and a new hope for you with this money. But be more prudent in managing your affairs this time!"

I was walking fast, and after all my bitterness and annoyance with them, I could sense in the streets a harbinger of change, inspiring a new expansiveness in my capacity for life: a feeling more like convalescence. There was a lightness in my limbs and a purity in my lungs, the likes of which I hadn't known since Sumaya's disappearance, as if I'd been saved on the point of suffocating. And oh how I wished Sumaya could have been with me at that moment, for us to wander the streets at night and explore the city in its hours of peaceful rest! I imagined I heard Sumaya's laugh, touched her body with mine, saw her eyes smiling in flirtatious innocence, then gazed at her as she turned round and round in her dance on the grass of our garden. Then I remembered her disappearance and said No, no, no…

In the Great Square, I saw the same prostitute who had propositioned me earlier, standing in the same corner, exhaustion now written on her face. I passed the cinema, deserted and dark as the grave; the alley that led to the Garden Cafe behind it; the basement window just above street level (and the calm, dark room within); and a branch of Shanoub stores. I finally reached the small cafe whose elderly owner Abu Hamed was still nodding off in the corner, as was his wont. A few men were there drinking coffee. I entered and ordered a cup, and before I left, told Abu Hamed that Inayat Hanem had died. It pleased me to learn that such news at that hour of night didn't mean a thing to my friend the old man!

I'd hardly crossed the café's doorstep when I heard thunder roar above the city. I reflected that the weather had been hot and sticky until then, that some rain could reinvigorate the city and cleanse the streets of the accumulated dust, and that I had to get home fast. But the thunder crashed again from the four corners of the sky, and minutes later, rain came hammering down, forcefully caressing my face and body. I didn't try to seek shelter from it at all. On the contrary, I was delighted to walk through sheets of rain strung like beads. I reached the house refreshed, even if I was wet, my clothes clinging to me like rags. At home I stripped off my wet clothes, dried myself, and went to bed.

I couldn't fall asleep at first. I listened to the rain running in streams around the house and saw an anonymous yellow flower floating on the water. Every one of its petals was moving and twisting (as if they were hands and legs) with joy, in supplication, in surrender. The flower floated downstream, turned in the bends, settled in the isolated corners, brushed up against the rocks, then slid down again, and reverted to turning round and round futilely. At the foot of the hill was a group of lovers in brightly colored clothing, and a rowboat waiting for the lovers to board it so it could carry them to Cythera, the island of Aphrodite. The yellow flower began floating around the rowboat. Then its petals opened and from them emerged Sumaya, her hair adorned with daisies, to steer the lovers' boat. The dream filled my vision, and then disaster overtook it when a deathly specter fell upon it. The flower's petals fell away, the lovers drowned in the river, and I remembered Roxane's request and that I must divorce Sumaya.

Chapter Eleven

Yet I felt Sumaya's body touching me, and dreamed I was stroking her lips and breasts with my hands, and that my fingers were playing with her hair, spreading it upon the pillow, and drawing a lock towards my eyes and lips. I heard her say, 'Two years, two whole years....' And I said, 'Ten years, twenty, fifty, why, why did you flee from me? Why?' And she said, 'I won't flee again, I won't flee, Amin.'

And again I ran my hand over the body lying next to me. What a wondrous fantasy! A real body. Is this how dreams come true?...Her belly...her waist...and suddenly I opened my eyes, and terror struck me. Every hair on my body stood up in fright, and I screamed at the top of my lungs, 'Sumaya!!' And the night was filled with my cry.

The reclining woman sat up and screamed, 'My love, Amin, Amin.'

She bent over to hug me. I thought she wanted to strangle me, so I grabbed her arms to free them from my neck, and I yelled, 'Who are you? Who are you?'

I jumped out of bed and turned on the light. The glare blinded me for a moment. My heart beat against my chest like ten hammers, sweat poured from my trembling body, and my mouth went dry.

Impossible, impossible. How many times had I spied a woman on the street and my heart jumped from thinking – if even for the briefest moment – that she was Sumaya. I saw Sumaya before me…sitting on my bed as she'd done in the past, almost naked, her hair spread in a wild halo around her face, where a bright pallor emphasized the height of her cheekbones and the wideness of her eyes. I hadn't realized her eyes were so wide.

'It's me, Amin. Me, me…were you scared?'

I approached her, still doubting she was real, and said, 'You terrified me. How did you get in?'

'I still keep a door key…two whole years.'

'Why didn't you wake me up?'

'But you kissed me in bed.'

'I thought I was dreaming.'

She laughed her silvery laugh I hadn't at all forgotten, and said, 'Come here…two whole years…on a night like this..'

She reached her arms towards me, and I didn't know whether to fall between them or to grab them and drag her from my room and throw her out. But I collapsed on the bed. She took my head in her hands and kissed me. 'I wronged you,' she said.

'What?' I asked.

I felt my determination flagging, for the terror had left me. I surrendered to her dewy lips and the light smell of her sweat, which I inhaled like perfume. My hands began to reacquaint themselves with the parts of her body. But she resumed, saying, 'My poor love. I wronged you.'

I realized then that she pitied me. The blood suddenly rushed to my head, my body rose up between her arms, and I yelled, 'You wronged me? You betrayed me. You cheated on me.' And I withdrew from her. So she approached me and dropped her femininity between my hands like a ripe fruit. But I pushed her away and said, 'Why did you come back?'

'Because I still love you.'

'You love me?'

I looked at her anew to be sure of her presence. There she was, after those long months that had passed like a suffocating night whose dawn would never break. And then I saw her for the first time. That accursed power in her eyes, that poisonous honey on her lips, that diabolic authority in her hands, all of which she worked upon me so I would fall wallowing upon her breast. Her face was emaciated, and her hair strewn upon it haphazardly. I remembered our first meeting between the trees, under the rain.

'You love me? You love me after you—'

'Do you still love me?' she interrupted.

The words shot out from between my teeth like a hiss. 'What a ridiculous question. Weren't you afraid I'd kill you if you returned?'

She gasped and yelled, 'Amin! Do you want to beat me?'

'God forbid! I wouldn't lay a finger on you…'

I got off the bed, stood above her, and added with all the coldness I could muster, 'Please leave.'

But she didn't budge from the bed. 'Don't you want to know why I left you, and why I returned?'

'Get out of my bed and leave,' I repeated.

'Don't you want to know?'

'What do I care about the reasons for your betrayal after all that's happened? You filled me with hate and scorn and anger at life. And despite all that, I was attached to you like a child to one of his dreams.'

'Then you still do love me!'

'Get out of my bed and leave.'

'Your bed is my bed.'

I fell upon her, grabbed her arms and, with all the power I could muster, dragged her and threw her to the ground. But she clung to my legs like a serpent trying to wrap itself around them. So I kicked her, bent over her, and began pushing her while she rolled on the ground yelling, 'I won't leave. I won't leave. I won't leave!'

At that moment I heard the concussion of a forceful explosion, making my teeth clack together and shaking the ground beneath my feet. I looked out the window, and the day had dawned, gray and clear; I hadn't even noticed. A few moments later, another explosion resounded, shaking the ground again. Through the window I saw on the horizon behind the houses and trees a column of smoke from which a colossal blaze emanated, waving back and forth and hurtling into the sky. I left Sumaya yelling and moaning on the floor. I went to the window to observe the hurtling flames that began twisting and rolling with expanses of smoke, then retreated for a moment only to burst forth into the air with the ferocity of beasts.

I could feel roiling flames colliding in my head as if they were a reflection of what I saw, sending me hurtling into a raucous laughter. I realized that what I saw was a purifying fire that broke out there to finish off contagious germs – it broke out to save me, to purify my flesh and blood. I stood fixed in the window, bewitched by what I saw. I would have liked to explode in continuous laughter like the thunder of successive explosions.

Then I heard a soft voice say, 'Amin. Amin.'

I remembered Sumaya sprawled across the floor. As I kept watching the columns of smoke rise and spread into the sky, I yelled, 'Get out, get out!'

'What were those explosions?'

'That was Roxane destroying her past.'

'Who's Roxane?'

'She's destroyed you, too.'

'What are you talking about?'

'That's Roxane burning her ancestors' infected clothes. Get out! Don't you see the fire? It's going to burn you too.'

'Amin, you've gone crazy!'

'No, I haven't! I've only now gotten my reason back.'

She pounced and clung to me, but I pushed her away, felling her again. She broke into tears and sobs while I turned to my clothes strewn upon a chair, quickly put on my shirt, pants and shoes, and headed towards the door. She had thrown herself across my path, so I jumped over her denuded body, and she screamed, 'You're crazy, you're crazy!'

I opened the door, turned towards her, and said, 'Why did you return and ruin everything for me? When you ran away, you forced me to wander the lethal labyrinths of the past. In your absence, I realized the extent to which I'd lost myself. Why did you return and ruin everything?'

Sobbing, she slunk towards me in the doorway. But I withdrew from her as if, in approaching me, she would infect me with a terrible disease, and I yelled, 'Once I yearned to embrace the most desirable woman on earth – but look at yourself: yellow like death, withered like death. And starting today, I want nothing to do with death!'

I hurried out to the iron gate, and from there to the road. The sun broke forth in a blaze that flooded the horizon. But I looked towards the rising columns of smoke in the distance, drawing me towards them over the city's hills, and I quickened my pace.

Suddenly a car sped towards me at an alarming rate before screeching to a halt in front of me.

'Did you hear?'

The words emerged in a merry voice from inside the car. I didn't need to look to recognize the person behind the steering wheel. 'Yes, Roxane, I heard.'

She opened the car door for me and said, 'Sit down next to me, then. I was just on my way to you.'

But I shut it gently and said, 'No. Thank you, Roxane, really. Your courage is admirable. You blew up your palace, saving yourself and me. But you have to search for your new life alone.'

'I was hoping you would come with me. Won't you change your mind?'

'No. Starting today, I no longer need to flee. She returned to me, but I escaped from her.'

'Who? Ah…that woman now leaving your house?'

I turned around to see Sumaya leaving from the gate and gazing at us from afar. 'Yes. Sumaya.'

Roxane started the car, which began to rumble and shake, and stared at Sumaya standing far away by my gate. Then she laughed and said, 'So you won't write our history?'

'It doesn't matter to me one bit!'

She extended her hand to shake mine and said, 'I want to send you a gift…the statue in the garden.'

'If it's still intact.'

'Goodbye!'

The car sped off with her.

When my eyes followed the car, I saw Sumaya walking up the road away from me. I turned from her and walked leisurely down the empty road.

But the road didn't remain empty for long. Only a short while later, the city streets stretched and branched out before me, filled with crowds of people. It wasn't hard, when I looked into their eyes, to realize that many of them were wandering aimlessly, just as I had for two long years, searching for an end to a long night and a beginning to a new life.

Arak*

'Take Khalil for instance. Does *he* ever hesitate to open his jaws to swallow a stream of money? An amazing image! Khalil, with his thick lips, and his moustache, more like an old toothbrush, shuts his eyes and opens his jaws – more and more, and suddenly, money gushes forth like dirt and settles in his throat and on his tongue, and then all of a sudden he's coughing, spitting, sputtering and cursing this and that man's honor, and wishing he could sink his dirty teeth into their women, honor and good name – all of 'em!

'I only slept three hours last night. I went to Fadila. Fadila! God forgive her parents. I'm gonna name my daughter Khati'a just so she'll be aware of her true essence.** I couldn't sleep 'cause I was thinking about virtue and vice. Where

_____

* Arak (*al-'araq*) is an alcoholic drink made from distilled grapes and flavored with aniseed. In Arabic, arak also means 'sweat.'

** Fadila means 'virtue' in Arabic, and Khati'a means 'sin.'

should we place Khalil, for example, on the spectrum of virtue and vice? What are the seven deadly sins, and which ones apply to him?

'But I wonder sometimes why I deal out judgments on people without first judging myself. That, at least, is a virtue I just *must* be graced with. I'll judge myself first, then others. Whoever's had the curse of the gods befall him, he'll see no harm in its befalling others. And the curse must fall – today, tomorrow, or the day after. So don't stick your nose up at me, because the curse will strike you too.

'A minute ago, I was just about to say: What do you care about me and my business for me to force it on you like this? You want to talk about Khalil, your dearest enemy and your fiercest friend. But my business is as important to you as it is to me. Because I lead and you follow. Because I let down the ladder for you, not for you to go up it – that would be impossible – but for you to go *down* it, lower and lower and lower. And I'll be there before you. I'll be there with the haters and the lovers, with those who spend their nights on the rooftops complaining about the moon and those who curse the doves in the morning for their loathsome cooing. What a pathetic man that was – the poet who mourned the cooing of the poor doves imprisoned in Baghdad, who didn't even mourn for the people:

> *In Bab al-Taq a collared dove cooed*
> *And drew out my copious, cascading tears**

'Or was he crying for his own imprisoned soul? Poor man. These days we don't cry. We roar and curse. That's why today at dawn, while I was in my bed on the roof, a dove landed near me, and I grabbed a glass of water on the bedside table and threw it at her with all my might. She flew away, cooing, and glass fragments covered the floor all around me. Five minutes later, I got out of bed, stepped on a piece of glass that slid into my foot ever so smoothly, and danced from the pain. What an idiot! How did I forget the glass shards that fast? But those doves really are annoying in the early morning. As if with their gloomy, continual cooing at dawn, they're warning you not to be too optimistic, reminding you that you're still descending the ladder. Rung by rung by rung.

'As I was saying, Khalil al-Safafiri doesn't turn up his nose where there's money involved. Thick skin, a hard head, a mill for a stomach. That's Khalil. He carries his university degree like a shield to ward off any accusation of being 'uncultured.' Culture? To him, culture is owning a house with ten rooms, a car and a few hundred stocks – and the rest will come. At that point, the rest will come obedient and willing: a wife

---

* Verses by the Tahirid governor of Khurasan, 'Abdallah ibn Tahir (798-844/5 CE. He pitied a particular turtle dove that he heard cooing in the Bab al-Taq neighborhood of Baghdad and paid 500 dirhams, a hefty sum, to buy it and set it free.

(a beautiful one, most likely), status (enviable, most likely), and…more money. You, my friend, must prepare yourself, like Khalil, to *act*, to *do* – not everything you're per*mit*ted to do, but everything it's *pos*sible to do. And to remember the difference.

'Khalil, in short, is a successful man. It could be said that he's gluttonous, greedy, stingy – but that's just the talk of the envious. But you – what do you do? You come to see me every day and tell me about your old friendship with Khalil. And you refuse to recognize that he's successful. Do his small eyes or large lips do him any harm? Soon he'll marry Umayma, and what will you do then? You'll sit here with me, in the cafe, and count the people coming and going, and I'll tell you how I slept with Fadila last night after I drank a quart of arak, and you'll tell me about a poem you wrote but were too shy to read aloud. When you write, you indulge yourself, Mustafa. Your imagination wraps itself around Umayma's legs, yet you write about her eyes. You wish you could pull her by the hair to the banks of the Tigris and wallow with her naked in the mud. Yet you write about a passion clean and pure, as if it didn't come from a merciless lust and an unyielding defeat. Fadila, my dear Mustafa, is waiting for you. And Fadila is pure in her own special way. She doesn't hold a university degree above her head to trick people into thinking she's cultured. Fadila is Fadila. Her existence is her essence, and vice versa. No flaws, no status, no houses, and no Chevrolet. Fadila's waiting for you at the bottom of the ladder.'

Mustafa Ahmad didn't say a word as his companion in the cafe burst with conversation. Sweat flowed slowly down Mustafa's forehead, which he wiped every now and then with the palm of his hand, his elbows leaning on the small iron table. Abbas didn't pay any attention to whether Mustafa was listening or not. Abbas had already drunk some arak at home, enough to burst out talking without caring whether anyone was listening, as long as *someone* sat there with him. Then Abbas had come to the cafe, where he'd found Mustafa sitting alone, reading a book about psychology. Abbas knew perfectly well that if he went there after ten at night, he would find Mustafa waiting for him, carrying two or three books, some of them in English, whose covers had been soiled by a hand covered liberally with sweat.

But Mustafa didn't say a word. It wasn't that his mind was elsewhere. On the contrary, he hung onto every word the alcohol exuded from between Abbas' lips. Abbas Jumaa Sirhan – graduate of the law school and an accountant in some government department, whose fingertips had been worn down from counting dinars, yet who was unable to put any of those coins into his own pocket.

Suddenly Mustafa stood and picked up the books from the small table. Abbas looked at him from his chair. 'Are you in a hurry?' he asked. 'Do you have work to do?'

Mustafa didn't answer, instead walking towards the door. He threw forty fils into the cafe owner's plate and went out to the road. Abbas caught up with him and walked alongside. 'Who can go to bed early in this weather?' Abbas asked. 'I don't sleep more than four or five hours these nights anyway. Want to come with me to the Acropolis? We haven't been there in a while. And I discovered a new brothel close by.'

'The Acropolis?' Mustafa asked. 'No. I'm going home.'

The Greek name rang in Mustafa's mind to the rhythm of their steps – acropolis, acropolis, necropolis. Necro-polis, the city of the dead, the dead, and thence to a new brothel, to a new Fadila, a new Virtue. Come in, make yourselves comfortable. Four girls. Saniya? She's actually busy now. But she'll be free in fifteen minutes. Fadila. Umayma's busy. Khalil's with her. But she'll be free in twenty years – perhaps then Khalil will have finished, and Umayma will be forty or forty-five, or fifty. And I'll still be waiting in the room outside. Incredible how she still looks like a young girl. She is what she is. Fadila. Her existence is her essence.

'Who could go home now?' Abbas continued. 'Our house is truly hellish. Not just in terms of the heat, but also in terms of who's in it. Whenever I go in, I'm not sure whether I'm one of its demons or a spirit being shoved inside from the world of the dead. Imagine, I got home last night at one in the morning…'

But Mustafa didn't hear the rest of Abbas' monologue, except for a few words whose meaning went unrecorded in his mind. He remembered the night before.

'God bless the sight of you!' Khalil said as if he really meant it,

standing up to shake his hand in the garden of the Lawyers' Club.

Mustafa turned into a big lump, exuding affection for two whole minutes. 'Who is it who's gotten too busy for the other, Khalil?' he asked.

'Really, Mustafa, I know I've been delinquent, but you know...'

'No, actually, I don't know. To disappear from us, or rather, to abandon us.'

'Only God knows men's hearts.'

Mustafa not only almost embraced Khalil, he almost kissed him on the cheek, and would have imbued his kiss with the warmth of a long friendship that went back to their childhood days. But he knew that starting a year ago or more, ever since he began working in business and politics at the same time, Khalil had 'changed'. Mustafa watched Khalil day by day grow more remote from him, until he reached that frightening distance expressed in a hard glance here and a chiding word there. But in that moment, he felt that the distance between them had vanished. And here they were, all of a sudden, as close as they used to be. The feeling didn't last more than a few seconds. A man Mustafa didn't know descended on them and shook Khalil's hand. 'Our congratulations!' he said. 'Well done!' He withdrew as Khalil thanked him.

'What's the congratulations for?' Mustafa asked. 'Seems like we never hear from you anymore.'

Khalil's features broadened. It looked like his face would go as wide as the building behind him from sheer happiness as his lips moved like hammers in opposite directions: 'Didn't you hear that I got engaged?'

'No, actually. To whom?'

'To Umayma. Umayma Othman al-Samawi.'

'Umayma?' Mustafa said, before the word could get stuck in his

throat. He felt his heart sink.

'Do you know her?'

'Ah...only by sight.'

By sight! It would have been more fitting of him to say, 'By her blood, by the undulations of her flesh and the folds of her brain. By her intestines, liver and gall bladder. Isn't that kind of knowledge deeper and stronger than knowledge of the tongue, of speech? And those poems he was too embarrassed to recite to anyone – are they not evidence of his knowledge of her? Hadn't he conversed with her for many long evenings, withdrawn and lonely in this or that cafe as he scribbled on pages whose every line she strolled over in her high heels? If that wasn't knowledge – oh! Only by sight!

'I've been working with her father for two years,' Khalil said, 'and now we're expanding our office.'

'So I heard.'

'Why don't you come visit us at the office?'

'I will.'

'Do you know the telephone number?'

'I'll find it in the directory.'

'Under the listing 'Othman al-Samawi – Office.' Come after six if you can; we're pretty busy throughout the day.'

Mustafa wished he could sink, fall into the depths of the earth where his face wouldn't be seen again. He felt as if Khalil were opening a door, beckoning him towards it, and saying: 'Be so kind as to leave now, and come back another time.'

'...And as usual, whenever I get home late at night, my mother clears her throat, just to prove she's been waiting up for me. But without uttering a word. Just clears her throat, as if to say: *Don't think I don't know where you've been…* Women don't miss a thing. We men are naive and innocent compared to women – *any* woman! – or even any *young* woman. Heat ripens women fast, just like it ripens fruit. Hey, Mustafa! Put that in one of your poems!

'*Rapidly the sun ripens Her, for what is Woman but a fruit…* Of course, the poetic meter is broken. But truth transcends rhyme and meter: Women are like fruit, their hearts are rotten, and men are like children who want to devour them. The worms hang down, stuck between their teeth, and their gullets remain rotten! I'm telling you, Mustafa: You've bitten into the fruit, and *I* can almost see the worms between your lips…'

The columns on Rashid Street cast their shadows on Mustafa's face as he walked along the edge of the covered sidewalk. Abbas, submerged in shadow and far from the light shining down the middle of the street, hadn't stopped talking. An impassioned panting came from the long arcade, joined every now and then by the blast of an intensely foul stench bestowed generously by the sewers.

'…And if I were you,' Abbas added, 'I'd spit those worms out in Khalil's face; then he could take them back to dear Umayma – return them to their source.'

Mustafa ran the palm of his hand over his forehead, temple and cheek, wiping away the glistening sweat. He felt as if the books were almost melting from the warmth and sweat of his other hand. 'But what's Umayma got to do with all this?' he asked.

Abbas fell upon the question to tear it apart. 'Umayma has *everything* to do with it! And if it weren't Umayma, it'd be Fatima, and if it weren't Fatima, then it'd be Inaam. One is all, and all is one – except for Fadila, of course. Fadila recognizes that she's made of clay: The sun strengthens her, then burns her, then cracks her until she collapses. But the others are mere fruit, and only a discerning eye can see the worms' way to their hearts. And here's the danger. The danger lies in being base, in dissimulating. The danger is in your seeing Khalil let go of every social bond and inhibition without you lifting a finger. Because he's preserved the appearance of social bonds, noble deeds and virtuous qualities… The danger is in your not seeing the woodworm's way into his heart.'

'But what's Umayma got to do with all that?'

'I just told you. Maybe you'll claim that Khalil doesn't know you love her, and that they're both heedless of you and unaware of your existence. Therein lies the error. Both of them carry your memory around like a burden on their hearts. And now, if you were to appear suddenly before Khalil, you'd see how he'd blanch, how his limbs would shake. And if you were to appear suddenly before Umayma, you'd see how she'd cover her face with her hands and rend your heart with tears.'

'But Khalil knows nothing of my relationship with Umayma.'

'I'm telling you, you're naive. And you don't believe me. Listen to the details, then. Two weeks ago – no, more, quite a bit more – anyway, a while ago, Khalil al-Safafiri came to me to collect one thousand three hundred fifty-seven dinars from the department. I served him a cup of tea, offered him a cigarette, and asked him how he was doing. He mentioned that he was about to get engaged. 'To whom?' I asked him. 'To Umayma,' he said. I asked him, 'For certain?' He said, 'Of course.' I didn't hesitate to throw the bomb in his face. I said, 'But don't you know that Mustafa Ahmad…lov…wants her, and has for a long time?' He said, 'Come on, leave off about that idiot.' He said it like it was a settled matter. Then he added, 'Of course I heard that he loves her. But now it'd be more honorable for him to have some shame, show some respect. Umayma knows about the matter and is very upset…"

'Umayma's very upset?'

'Very upset…'

And all at once, Mustafa was at Khalil's doorstep. The house was dark, and when he rang the doorbell, then pressed again and held it, no one answered him. He stood in place, dripping sweat. Then Khalil arrived in his Chevrolet, stopped at the gate, and got out. Mustafa approached him with steady paces, descending the two steps that led down from the entrance to the house. Khalil started, retreated, and gripped the two panels of the iron gate. Then he uttered, 'Oh…Mustafa…you scared me!'

'Is that right?'

'Let's go inside. You must have something important to tell me. Why else would you have come at this hour?'

'I do have something important. But we won't go inside. In fact, you'll never enter your house again.'

'Mustafa, what are you talking about?'

Mustafa raised two clenched fists. 'What did you say about me regarding Umayma?' he asked.

Khalil's voice stuck in his throat for a moment until it came out in a dry rasp. 'I didn't…say…anything…'

'Is Umayma upset with me?'

'I didn't say anything…I swear.'

Mustafa's hands were raised, his fingers outstretched, each one of them transformed into hard, unbending steel. 'Umayma's upset with me?' he asked. Khalil retreated, descending the step to the gate, his eyes bulging. His back struck the car while Mustafa stepped towards him with small, fixed, evil paces. Then at last he fell upon his neck with both hands and pressed his thumbs into his throat, squeezing with strength and violence until he heard his larynx crack, his head fell to the side, and he sank to the ground motionless.

With the palm of his hand, Mustafa wiped away the sweat on his forehead and with total calm returned to Rashid Street.

'Mustafa! Are you listening?'

'Huh?'

'I asked you, do you want to go down this alley with me?'

'Why?'

'I know a place here, with girls. I haven't been in a long time.'

'What? A place? Ah, I see. No. No.'

'What's with all this hesitation?'

'Because if I'm not drunk, Abbas, I can't even look at those kinds of women.'

Abbas laughed like a man who's won a game after a great struggle. He patted Mustafa's shoulder. 'Why don't you talk?' Abbas asked. 'Why don't you say something?' He patted his shoulder again.

But Mustafa felt that Abbas was crushing him with his affectionate pats. He shook his shoulders to throw off his touch.

'I'll help you forget Umayma right now,' Abbas added. 'But be quick, before Abu Boutros closes for the night.'

Mustafa returned to himself as he strode with wide, hastening steps. 'Two or three days ago,' he said, 'a man killed his wife in our street with a cane. He attacked her head with it, and she fell where she stood, her skull split open.'

It seemed Abbas had noticed the hidden connection between this sudden memory and what was going on in Mustafa's mind, as he said, 'A cane – that's nothing. A few days ago a man killed his wife with an axe. Imagine: He gripped the axe and brought it down on her head, her neck, her stomach – on every part of her body, as if she were a tree he was cutting down. He left her limbs scattered about.

Then, proud as a lion, he turned himself into the police. He accused her of adultery. Did everyone get all hot and bothered? No. The murderer was sentenced to three years in jail, and his honor was wiped clean.'

'A terrible thing.'

'Why? Woman has been an object of doubt since the dawn of history. The worm is in her heart. While it works within, it waits to poison the man who sinks his teeth into her. If you see the worm, you have to exterminate it before it can cast its eggs into your mouth and throat. The sun, which ripens fruit, also speeds up the reproduction of worms.'

'You're stretching the truth with these symbols of yours.'

'I consider Umayma unfaithful.'

'Please don't mention her again.'

'I consider Khalil unfaithful too.'

'Enough! God damn it!'

'Never mind. In the Acropolis, one can forget truths and symbols. And if I were you, I'd consider the truth greater than symbols. If one can forget symbols, one can't forget the truth.'

'But what's correct is precisely the opposite of that. In order *not* to forget truths, we preserve their essence by condensing them into symbols.'

Abbas laughed and said, 'You probably got that from the psychology book you're reading. Do you know the eternal truth that everything in existence points to? He who reads a lot won't succeed in life. That's the first truth. How many books does Khalil al-Safafiri read in a year? The second truth is that young men like you rush towards delusions and know nothing about availing themselves of the truth. What have you gotten from Umayma besides a stolen kiss a year ago, or more?'

kiss kiss kiss kiss

'*Do you love me that much?*'

Mustafa ran his fingers through her hair and whispered, 'Don't talk – they'll hear us.'

Then he hurried to close the door and turned on the tap to delude any sudden arrival into thinking someone was washing up in the bathroom – so that they wouldn't come in, so that the sound of water, rushshshshshsh…would cover up the sweet cooing and the crackle of kisses…

The rest of the guests were clamoring about in the living room, drinking tea. Then a few of them got up to put a record on to dance to. Mustafa pressed Umayma to his chest in the bathroom, his fingers planted in her flesh, her arms wrapped tightly around his neck, and both their mouths worn out from kissing.

Then Umayma said, 'You've eaten off all my lipstick…how can I go out now with my lips like this?' She studied her face in the mirror above the sink.

At that moment, a cry arose from the faraway foyer: 'Mustafa, Mustafa! Where's Mustafa?'

He immediately snuck out of the bathroom to the rear door and from there to the garden, and from there –

They entered the long, narrow arcade, dazzlingly lit,

which led them to the garden with its faint colored lights. It was filled with the sounds of drinkers, laughers, and the discontent. Abu Boutros slunk towards them from a corner like a leopard in the jungle and said, 'Welcome, welcome, Abu Fadel. After me, please.' He cut them a path through the atmosphere, filled with the mirth of arak, and sat them at a table almost hidden under the dense cover of a tree. Each of them ordered half a quart of arak.

Abbas resumed talking. 'Just like I told you. People like you will accept delusion—'

But he was surprised when Mustafa cut him off, saying, 'And you, Abbas, don't you embrace delusions day and night?'

'Me? I'm a realistic man. Delusions don't carry me away, and appearances don't deceive me. I pursue only the truth.'

'Like Fadila, for instance?'

'Like Fadila for instance. And I know her price exactly.'

Suddenly a silence settled between them. For the first time that night, they exchanged glances, until the waiter brought the drinks, the ice, and the mezze. In order to clear a space for them on the table, he moved Mustafa's books to the side and withdrew. They began pouring the water in the arak and adding pieces of ice. Then Abbas took a large draught from his glass and said, 'I know the exact price of Khalil and Umayma too.'

Mustafa felt the blood rush to his head. 'That's enough!' he yelled. 'Haven't you gotten tired of talking about them?'

Abbas was taken aback by such sudden anger and rapidly gulped down what remained in his glass. 'Take it easy,' he said. 'Why are you upset? What still exists between you and Khalil, or you and Umayma, for you to be so angered by what I'm saying? I know their exact price because I see them with my eyes, and not yours. And I want *you* to see them with my eyes, so you can see the truth of your situation—'

'With your eyes? You only see depravity and whoredom.'

'To the pure man, everything is pure! Ha ha!'

'Depravity and poverty. They're connected by a sinister bond, and we must get rid of them both.' So said Khalil as he and Mustafa walked arm in arm on the high road overlooking the clay houses, concatenated and clustered. Small hills of cowpies surrounded them all, while the tiny dark frames of naked children ran here and there, then sat down in the dirt as the flies sucked at the fluid discharge in their eyes.

'We have to read a lot,' Mustafa said, 'in order to understand the meaning of poverty, to know how to treat it.'

'A college education won't be enough for us,' Khalil said. 'We have to read all kinds of books, especially after we graduate.'

'We'll read, write and work in order to eradicate this poverty and depravity.'

A dog shot out of a hut towards them and began barking and barking, incessantly barking, as if he knew no meaning to his existence apart from barking his throat out.

Mustafa heard Abbas. 'And here you are,' he said, 'sitting on a chair in a cafe reading psychology books.' Abbas reached his hand towards the books on the table, 'And you can't even see yourself, like an insect buzzing about the trash…depravity and whoredom!'

Abbas then threw the books to the ground.

Darkness descended on Mustafa's eyes, and an almighty determination broke out in his limbs, destroying all his willpower. He found himself gripping the table and flipping it over, along with all its contents, onto Abbas's front. Abbas lost his balance and fell to the ground before he could realize what had happened. Mustafa raised a chair with his powerful hands and brought it down upon his friend's head as he was trying to get up, shouting, 'Mustafa! Mustafa!' Between his lips Mustafa uttered foul curses that repeated ceaselessly. But a group of drinkers took hold of Mustafa from behind and pinned his arms, so he began kicking about with his feet to strike Abbas while he tried to get up. He managed to strike him once or twice in the chest with the tip of his shoe until the drinkers dragged him away towards the arcade. The scent of mastika and alcohol on their breath filled Mustafa's lungs. Abu Boutros began fluttering about in the hubbub, helpless and afraid, for drunkards' fights always cost him an old chair here and a split table there. But as soon as Mustafa had been removed, Abu Boutros saw to Abbas and helped him stand up. He began wiping the fava beans, tomatoes, and the rest of the mezze off Abbas' front with a towel. Abbas' pants and white shirt had gotten embarrassingly wet. He could feel the wetness between his thighs, and sweat exuded from inside his shirt.

Mustafa turned his back to the garden, entered the long narrow arcade, and took his handkerchief out of his pocket to wipe away the stream of sweat from above his eyebrows, between his eyes, and around his neck. Yet when he reached the door, he felt that he'd forgotten something, though he couldn't exactly remember what, and began groping about in his pockets. Then he turned around and walked through the arcade, returning to the garden. Two servers blocked his way, and one of them said, 'What, do you want the police to show up?'

But he pushed them aside and walked over to a group of men that had gathered around Abbas. They were babbling about what had happened, but upon seeing him return, they immediately fell silent. Mustafa bent over the three books scattered on the ground, which the men milling about had trampled on during the fight, and picked them up one by one without meeting anyone's eyes. He raised his hand to his forehead to wipe away the ooze of sweat once more. And then he returned to the arcade with the dazzling lights, which he left for the night and the long road.

Singer in the Shadows

Ala dalouna, ala dalouna...
Dalouna, dalouna, dalouna, clapping, trilling and dalouna

The oud player was enraptured by his song and his drink, which made him hang his head down over his oud as the pick between his fingers struck the strings. The strings struck back with a hum that rose and fell among the singers' voices.

The hands clapped and clapped, *Ala dalouna, and the north wind* –

The sun's rays danced about on the olive trees.

Dusty green trees stood one after the other on the terraces of the mountain sloping down to the road. Perhaps the selfsame olive trees were planted by saints in olden times, for those gnarled, twisted trunks with all their cracked gray bark are the sisters of time and of days long past. When

Selloum thought about them, he felt a delightful dizziness, as if he were approaching the confluence of the earth and sky beyond those far blue hills.

Ooooof, yaba... The sun's rays danced about on thousands of olive leaves, green and dusty to the touch, whose fragrance was that of the land, the land on one of whose rocks he sat, for rocks were everywhere: whitened and greened, and who knows what hand had scattered them upon these slopes that rolled down towards a wide, distant valley.

The men, women and children were singing and striking their palms together, glasses of arak before the old men, who sat cross-legged in the reticulate shadows beneath the thin branches, singing *Ala dalouna*, then stopping to hold their breath and stay their voices while the oud player sent forth a sigh of *Oooooof...* a sigh as long as the days of old, charged with the past's – the entire past's – longing for loved ones whom the eye can no longer see, and sorrow for the loved ones who've departed, their rosy lips and cheeks no longer to be kissed... *Oooooof...* Dear sorrow...! And Selloum listened, understanding and not understanding, the song causing longing and sorrow to gush forth, even from his seven years. But when he grows up like those men and, like them, sits cross-legged under the olive trees on holidays, he'll harbor the power and reverence that those men do, their longing and their sorrow.

Oooooof... The glass passed among the men as a woman began serving more pieces of bread, white cheese and green olives...

Selloum salivated, not only from seeing the appetizers but also from the smell of rice and meat wafting from a large pot over the fire behind the singers. In that pot lay the fulfillment of a promise his friend Mousa had made him. Where was Mousa now?

Selloum turned about himself, searching for his friend among the group of clappers and singers, among the women moving tirelessly under the nearby olive tree, among the heaps of baskets and bundles and plates. He couldn't find him. When he turned to look at the distant pot, around which had gathered a number of young boys and two or three women, breaking sticks and feeding them to the fire, one of them coughing every now and then when a gust of wind blew smoke in her face – there, he saw Mousa sitting on a rock, his eyes fixed on the pot. Selloum was reassured and returned to singing, clapping two or three times and then stopping. His eye caressed the pot, distant and smoking, and the heady smell of rice and meat – even if sometimes mingled with smoke or the faint smell of trees and dirt – tickled his throat.

As he sat on his rock he felt something dry pressing into his thigh, something that protruded from his pocket. It almost fell out, but Selloum grabbed it fast with one of his clapping hands and pushed it deep into his pocket so that no one would see: a crust of bread. It wouldn't be proper for everyone to see that object in his hands in such a place, with the mouthwatering food just about ready.

Ooooooooh... Selloum wished he too had the courage to raise his voice with the phrase of the *mejana*.* How often had he sat in the company of Mousa and Ilyas and others on the threshold of a closed shop in the small town's streets to stage a night of song. Each one of them would bend his arms as if embracing an oud and pretend to play. Then they would begin singing *Ala dalouna*, and Selloum would follow it up with a long, drawn-out *Oooooof*. He didn't know many of the words following those sighs, so he confined himself to:

> The camels are loaded
> The camels are loaded, and the bells are ringing
> *ya layli ya layl*

And each and every time he would imagine the camels with their arched necks and haughty heads pumping back and forth, and their yellow bells, bells within bells, ringing all along the dusty road that led from his town to the distant olive trees and the city beyond the hills, that magical city he once beheld as he walked there with his father, its lofty walls towering over the cars and peddlers, people shouting and sitting in the cafes outside Jaffa Gate.

---

* Arabic popular poetry sung at weddings, holidays and celebrations in the Levant and northern Iraq.

'Tomorrow's the Feast of St. George.'

Mousa had said that to Selloum the previous afternoon, reminding him of what he'd said many times before: 'There'll be lots of people there. Abu Ilyas vowed that if Ilyas recovered, he'd slaughter a sheep. And Ilyas got better. Have you seen the sheep they bought a few days ago?'

'Yes,' Selloum said. 'Didn't we take him a bagful of grass from the fig gardens? So, they'll slaughter him tomorrow?'

'Yes. And they'll cook him with rice. And give his meat away to people. They're going to sing for a while after finishing their prayers; then they'll cook the food.'

'Can we go to the Feast?'

'Of course. And we'll eat rice and meat.'

Selloum's dinner that night with his parents and brothers was lentil soup. When he found out, Selloum said to his mother, 'Ugh, lentils again? I'm sick of lentils.'

His mother said, 'What do you want? Roast chicken?'

'No. Just a bit of meat.'

'Meat during the week, you little gourmand? How about I cook you a lamb's head and lamb's feet on Sunday.'

'Ugh, I'm sick of heads and feet. I want a little meat.'

'What you want is a good hiding! Your father works from dawn to dusk, and he doesn't say things like that.'

'Why don't you buy us a little meat?'

'What would I buy it with? The lice on your head?'

'Tomorrow I'm going to the Feast of St. George,' said Selloum, leaving the matter in God's hands. 'Abu Ilyas swore he would slaughter a sheep to celebrate his son's recovery. There'll be a lot of meat there.'

In the early morning, Selloum awoke to the sound of his mother and father talking, his mother walking back and forth in her slippers slapping the bare floor of the room. He threw off the tattered blanket, which he would draw up to his chin when he slept. Suddenly Mousa appeared at the door, bashful and wary, to send his shrill voice inside. 'Let's go, Selloum! Are you still not up?'

Selloum got up and threw on his pants and shirt.

'But I still haven't had a chance to patch your ripped pants!' his mother said. Then she turned to his brothers sleeping on the ground, one after the other. 'We'll never catch up with the rest of them,' she said to his father. 'Selloum's pants have only lasted a month. But the little devil climbs trees and rolls in the dirt and has no mercy on his clothes.'

Selloum sensed intangibly the large patch on the seat of his pants, which his mother had torn from a worn pair of his older brother's.

After washing and eating breakfast, Selloum and Mousa left for the yard, up from there to the fig garden, and from there to the road. Suddenly Selloum realized that Mousa was wearing shoes. 'You know, my mom didn't catch me leaving barefoot,' he said. 'I hate shoes. But she makes me wear them on Sundays and holidays.'

'Wait here a minute,' Mousa said, 'I'll go back home and take off my shoes too. But I'm afraid my mom'll see.'

He dashed off to a nearby house. Selloum suddenly remembered something and ran back to his house too. 'Why'd you come back?' his mother asked.

He headed towards the bread basket. 'I want a piece of bread,' he replied.

He took a crust of bread baked three or four days before and stuffed it in the little pocket of his pants, making it swell. He returned to the fig garden and from there to the road again. A moment later, Mousa arrived, barefoot like him, and they dashed off towards St. George's Monastery as if they were going to the land where joys never end, their feet getting whiter and whiter from the accumulating dust.

Oooooooof... The dust on the olive branches almost quaked from the reverberations of the singer's lone sigh as it stretched and twisted around the men, women and children, growing in ripples that encompassed the shadows, the radiant sun and the olive trees stretching into the distance and, below them, the festivalgoers.

The smoke beneath the large pot rose gradually with the melody, before vanishing in strands like streams of longing set to music. Selloum recalled the only song he knew:

> The camels are loaded.
> And the bells are ringing.

He pushed his bare feet into the earth, feeling the moist cold in the depths of the soil. He imagined that bells were ringing from afar.

Umm Ilyas came and called out to the men, 'All right, now, men, your turn!'

The singing suddenly stopped, and the oud player strummed the strings two or three more times before he took notice. Then he slipped the pick between the strings on the oud's neck and set it aside.

A moment later, the mat was spread out, the clatter of plates filled the air, and the cries of women and men rose as they arranged the table.

'A plate here, a plate there, a plate for Abu Sameer. Come on, Abu Wadea, bread, spoons, spoons!' The spoons fell on the flattened mat with a sharp ring – a sound pleasing to the hungry. Then the women began bringing the rice on large trays topped with cuts of meat and putting them on the mat before the men. Hands reached towards the trays, spoons emptied the trays' contents onto plates, and a number of children flocked to the mat. 'Children!' Umm Ilyas shouted, 'you all come later. The children come later. Men come first. Where did all those kids come from anyway? Goddammit!' Some of the children retreated to wait for the second helping. Umm Ilyas called out, addressing the men, 'Eat up, men, for health and strength. Look alive there, Abu George. Come on, y'all, fix him another plate. Give Abu Abdallah a thigh there...'

From his rock, Selloum saw Abu George, his globular head drooping over his belly, which was fixed firmly in his lap. Abu George lifted the rice to his open maw, much of it getting caught on his moustache and the sides of his mouth. He pushed the rice between his lips with a piece of meat on a bone that he gripped in his hand, tearing the meat off it with his powerful teeth. Abu George's plate was filled again. Selloum's feet sank into the moist earth.

Some children approached the table again. One of the men yelled at them, 'Get back! Wait a minute!'

One of the women came and dispersed them, and they fell back like a frightened flock of chickens. One of them, as he was retreating, tripped over Selloum, who was sitting on the rock with his feet planted in the mud. When the other boy saw him, Selloum felt shame, which he tried but failed to overcome. He suddenly stood up and retreated from his seat two or three steps.

'Let's go, ladies!' Umm Ilyas cried out to the women, and they came again, carrying plates of rice. Yet the plates were less full than before, and the pieces of meat that crowned them were sparser. The men got up one after the other to pour water over their hands with jars and jerry cans while the women took their places and the children gathered around the plates.

Selloum felt an overpowering hunger, as if an abyss had split open in his stomach, revealing a void that demanded to be filled. So he got up from his place and stepped towards the food.

'Where did all these kids come from?' Umm Wadea yelled. 'Don't they have any shame?' She pushed two children who looked unfamiliar to her. Selloum was behind them, and they bumped into him. When he was pushed forward by the others, Umm Wadea's open palm struck him to turn him away. 'Damn you!' she said. 'Child after child! Go back home to your own mothers! What is this ruckus?'

Selloum then felt as if the abyss in his insides had closed. He saw Mousa bent over the rice, his hand stuffing his face. But the woman's shove made Selloum fall back. He turned from the sight of the food and felt as if someone were kicking him in the behind and driving him away like a dog. His walk over the dirt between the rocks and trees was slow at first. Then he began to accelerate, eventually running, without knowing where he was going at such speed. But he understood that he didn't want to hear the sounds of people eating behind him.

When he reached the monastery, he walked to the other side of the old building, in whose shadow ran a spring where the festivalgoers would come to fill up their jars and jerry cans before returning to sit under the shade of the trees.

He sat on a rock and felt an intense desire to cry but was determined not to. Then he got the crust of bread out of his pocket, shook off the dust that clung to it and closed his teeth around it. It had become as hard as a bone, and he couldn't tear a bite from it. The roof of his throat was dry.

He approached the spring, leaned over it, and let the water flow over the bread until it was wet on both sides. All the while, he felt the water shooting back and forth, cold and refreshing, over his feet and shins, carving arabesques in the dust on them. He stood up, extended his legs into the gentle flow, and chewed the wet bread as he watched his feet get cleaner and cleaner.

Then he doused his bread again and walked to a nearby rock, his feet dripping with water. He sat down to eat his lunch and said to himself, 'Good thing I brought some bread with me...'

After a while, he heard a group of singers behind him. Clapping, trilling. A new song he hadn't heard before. He turned around towards the singers and remembered again the words of his song:

'The camels are loaded...'

Then he said out loud, 'Loaded...with what?' He imagined the camels loaded down with bags swollen from their contents, without knowing what was in them. Suddenly Mousa descended in his direction, yelling, 'Selloum!'

He wolfed down the last bite he was then chewing so that Mousa wouldn't find out what had happened. 'Don't you want to wash your feet?' he asked.

'Did you eat?' Mousa asked.

'Yes.'

'Did you eat meat?'

'Of course.'

'I only got a small piece.'

'It's all the same,' Selloum said. 'Big or small.' Mousa headed towards the spring and drank from it. He washed his feet, returned to his friend, and sat down next to him on the rock.

The Gramophone

Yusuf grasped the zinc ingot and fed it into the jaws of the vice, which he tightened. Then he took a long file and set it on top of the ingot. Before he started to burnish it, he turned to me. 'Do you hear that, Yacoub?' he asked.

'Yes,' I said. I stepped over a pile of zinc pieces to glance in the crucible, shimmering from the metal slowly melting in the middle of the blazing furnace.

'Do you hear it, Yacoub?' Yusuf repeated. 'Relax a bit. You're still young, so don't overexert yourself. Foreman Hanna's busy.' He winked to indicate how busy the foreman was, then extended his thumb and forefinger as if he were holding a glass between them, and raised them to his lips with an expressive gesture. 'The foreman's busy,' he said, 'and oh how I wish I were with him now! Ah, if you only knew, Yacoub, about my life in Egypt, five years ago. Five years that changed my life. Every evening I'd put on an elegant, ironed suit and a starched white shirt and go to a cafe or a bar with a few friends. Then we'd go to a cabaret... money...money, as much as the soul desires. Drink, laughter and women...five years that changed my life...'

Then he set the file on the ingot and proceeded to polish it, singing to the rhythm of the file. I was enchanted by his singing, as he was, and every so often his hands would stop working while he drew out his voice with a tune that trembled in his throat, ascending to a peak of elation and descending to a rasp of pain. It seemed like his eyes had filled with tears. Then his hands resumed working, and he returned to filing and hammering. 'Five years, from glory to disgrace,' he said. 'By God, this isn't living, Yacoub...money and friends and women. Light-skinned girls and dark-skinned girls, tall and short. Praise the Lord for such wondrous variety.'

He cautiously removed a pack of cigarettes from his breast pocket, took one out, and returned the pack to his pocket. He lit the cigarette and exhaled the smoke, his hand on the vice, his stray glances recalling his glory days through the wisps of smoke.

'Please, Yusuf,' I said, 'take a look at the crucible. Should I put some more zinc pieces in?'

He eyeballed it from where he was standing and said, 'Damn the crucible. I told you, the foreman's busy. He'll be very late today. Did you prepare all the molds in the sand?'

'Yes,' I said. 'They're all ready.'

All of a sudden, the foreman, Hanna al-Mawasiri, appeared unexpectedly, trying to conceal the stagger in his gait. But his mirth was obvious, and as soon as he stepped over the threshold of the workshop, he yelled, imitating an Egyptian accent, 'Hey there, prince! You filed it all, I hope? You think I don't know you, prince? I kneaded you and baked you like a loaf of bread, boy… Can't turn my back for five minutes without you slacking off…' He sat on the edge of the sand that we used for making molds to melt the metals in. Hanna turned to me. 'God help Yusuf,' he said. 'A young man who's getting old. Look, look, Yacoub, look!' Then he lowered his voice, brought his mouth, reeking of alcohol, close to my ear and whispered, 'But make sure he doesn't catch you looking! Haha, haha. God help you, Yusuf.'

That is to say, Yusuf's pants were torn and patched from top to bottom, front and back, and no one, not even Yusuf himself, could remember their original color. They had faded, been soiled, and turned into disparate shreds unconnected to each other except by force of will, and Yusuf's leather belt held them up on his waist. But the rips in the crotch of his pants were constantly widening, and the patches failed to cover them. Hanna would alert me to spy, through the patches, Yusuf's drooping genitals. 'Three hundred pounds I spent in two months,' Yusuf said. He stopped filing for a moment. 'By God, Hanna, three hundred pounds in two months…' And he withdrew to his filing.

'Dream on,' Hanna said, 'dream on, prince, dream on, cap'n. But flex those muscles for some work. We have to pour these molds before evening.' Then he turned to me and said, 'Are the molds ready?'

'Yes, sir,' I said.

Despite his intoxication, Hanna cast an expert glance at the squares in the brown sand, and his eyes moved from one mold to another. Then he got up, looked at the flaming crucible, stripped off his jacket, rolled up his sleeves, unbuttoned his shirt, and said, 'Let's go, Yusuf!'

The process of pouring molten zinc took us about a quarter of an hour. But the exertion of that fifteen-minute period amounted to that of all the other hours of the workday. I watched the veins on our arms nearly burst as we lifted the crucible with the long horizontal tongs. The sweat dripped from our faces and ran in streams that sometimes poured into our eyes. Whenever a mistake or a poor estimate occurred while casting into the mold's holes, we would curse, and curse again, for it lightened the intensity of the strain our bodies suffered from head to toe.

When we finished our task and put the crucible in a corner to cool, it looked to me like Hanna had sobered up. He took a scrap of cloth and wiped his forehead and face while Yusuf sat on a crate to rest and dry his forehead too. Then he said, 'What do you all think about something for dinner?'

But Hanna, without uttering a word, picked up a piece of soap and headed towards the far corner, where we kept a clay jar filled with water. He scooped a bowlful from it and proceeded to wash his hands and face.

'Go and buy me a plate of tripe,' Yusuf said. From a pocket near the belt of his pants, he took out a penny and gave it to me. Suddenly Hanna, soap suds still on his face and neck, yelled, 'Here, Yacoub, take another penny and buy yourself something to eat too.' He wiped his right hand cursorily over the towel, then stuck it in his pocket, and extracted a penny.

I walked up from the neighborhood of al-Jora, the Hollow, to the Nabi Dawood Overlook, where a cook from Hebron was preparing stuffed tripe in two huge cauldrons on an outdoor wood fire. The smell of the broth, with its garlic, pepper, and lemon, not to mention the smell of the tripe itself, attracted the hungry in spite of themselves. So he was always surrounded by a crowd of blacksmiths from the Hollow, laborers, donkey drivers, and automobile drivers – some of them squatting, some of them sitting on the ground, and some of them standing – with plates of tripe in their hands and the air filled with its fragrance. As the cook was ladling up a stomach with a quantity of stew, measuring it cautiously and pouring it into the deep dish, I stepped up to order two plates. I spotted Abed al-Aawar, the magazine seller, with a bundle of his wares next to him. He saw me immediately and called out, 'Have you gotten the latest issue of *Dunya*?'

I made my way towards him and said, 'No. Has it arrived?' Like a magician conjuring a fruit from his sleeve, he took out a copy of Dunya from a bundle of magazines and offered it to me. When I received it, smelled its new ink, and saw its many pictures, I didn't know whether to return it to him and buy a plate of tripe for myself with the penny that I had, or to add half a penny to it, buy the magazine, and let my mouth salivate in vain…

'I'll take it!'

I took the magazine and handed him the amount, one and a half pennies. I returned to the cook and said, 'One plate of tripe!'

With his practiced skill and caution, the cook scooped up the appropriate quantity, poured it in a bowl, and handed it to me. 'Just return the bowl soon,' he said.

I descended from the Overlook to the foundry, balancing the plate in my hands so as not to spill its precious stew, the mouthwatering magazine under my arm.

'Do you have a brain in that head of yours, boy? Do you?' said Yusuf, sitting on the wooden box.

'Where's the foreman?' I said.

'The foreman's gone.' He reenacted the movement of raising the glass to his lips. 'Did you come back with a magazine again instead of a plate of food?'

'Here you go.'

He took the plate and got a spoon from between the files

and hammers and wiped it off with his thumb. As I turned the pages of the magazine eagerly and he slurped at his broth, he said, 'Are you in love or something, Yacoub? Do you feed your mind, or your stomach? How do you expect to put on weight and get stronger, and at your age, if you buy magazines with every penny you get – useless magazines that, unlike this delightful tripe, won't fatten you up?'

But I didn't answer him, having occupied myself with turning the magazine's pages, reading the articles' titles, and examining the pictures. While I gave him only half my attention, he continued, 'Strength lies in your arm. And in the future, that arm is the only thing that'll help you. Do you see me here wearing these rags, and think I haven't known luxury and wealth? With this hand, I made hundreds of pounds. I was a real prince, Yacoub.' In an Egyptian accent, Yusuf said, '*That's what the prince wants!* – that's what everyone around me said whenever I wanted something. Strength lies in this arm. But…women, blonde women and black women, music and song, moonlit nights, late nights with the… You're still young, my boy. May God save you from rouged lips, eyes made up with kohl and mascara, and arched eyebrows.'

He slurped from his spoon again and again, took the stuffed tripe in his fingers, and sank his teeth into it, as his words impeded the task at hand. But I interrupted him, saying, 'Here's an article with the title 'Chamber Music in the Eighteenth Century.''

'Music can be dangerous if you don't watch yourself,' he said, 'especially if you can sing. Oud players, qanoon players, violinists, they'll gather around you, a kohl-eyed beauty sitting in your lap, and the cup goes round, and the night wind blows on the fire in your heart…'

Suddenly he put the food aside and beat his chest with his fist. 'This cursed heart, this bastard – it isn't reasonable, and it won't behave until its owner keels over. You're still young, Yacoub. But you'll hear your elders say, 'Women are all the same. In the end there's no difference between one and another.' Lies, lies, lies! Every woman has her own taste and flavor. Each one of 'em's a dish that's different from the others. And none of them is enough. Don't be fooled by these rags covering my body, Yacoub. By God, I've seen my share of life—'

He stopped talking, and I raised my eyes from the magazine to find him looking towards the door. I turned my eyes in the direction of his. I saw a woman strolling leisurely by, and she looked in the foundry as if searching for someone inside. Her cheeks were as red as a rose, but her forehead and the rest of her face were as white as flour, and the kohl around her eyes was thick. She continued her swaying, rolling gait upon her high heels, a leather purse in her hand. Yusuf hurried to the door, gazing at her as she got farther and farther away, her behind jiggling and swaying.

Finally Yusuf said, 'Do you know who that was?'

'No.'

'That was Subhiya.'

'Subhiya?'

'God help the foreman! Right now she's going to Abu Shlomo's store, where Hanna's waiting for her... Abu Shlomo gives Hanna arak in the back room, the room connected to the rear of the store, and after that – goddamn you, Hanna! May the Lord protect us, and this foundry.'

He again removed his pack of cigarettes from his breast pocket, took a cigarette from it, and returned the pack with caution. He lit the cigarette, and as he exhaled the smoke from his mouth and nostrils, he said, 'Just like I told you. Every woman has her own taste and flavor. Praise the Lord for such wondrous variety!'

The next morning Yusuf didn't come to the foundry. We had to prepare new molds for copper ingots, which were a bit complicated. Foreman Hanna began digging the previous day's ingots out of the sand as he repeated, 'So this means the prince isn't coming, so this means he isn't coming? Sunk in his dreams while we have work to do. We have responsibilities, we have debts to pay...so this means he's not coming?' Finally, Hanna said to me, 'Go to his house, and drag him out by the ears!'

Yusuf's 'house,' as far as I knew, was on a road near the workshop. Whenever we left work in the evenings, I'd see him entering a wooden gate between the blacksmiths' shops. He would disappear behind it and never invite anyone to visit him. I opened the gate and entered it with a great deal of circumspection. I didn't see a house in the area, but I did see a staircase in an unfinished building. The stairs led to a raised platform built against the wall, with nothing above it save the sky. On one end of the platform stood a wooden hut, only slightly larger than a doghouse, its boards uneven and out of joint. The nails protruded from them all over the place like small daggers, signs of the many other uses to which the boards had been put in the past.

I went up to the platform and called out, 'Yusuf, Yusuf!'

A feeble, morose voice answered me. 'Who is it? Come in.' The 'door' was an old piece of sack. I raised it and saw Yusuf stretched out under a tattered, blackened blanket, a jar of water lying nearby along with some tin plates, a Primus stove, and several empty bottles, some of them lying on their sides. But my eyes suddenly fixed on a pile of records near a blue box, which I immediately realized was a gramophone. There didn't appear to be any connection between the person covered in rags and the gramophone with its records.

Yusuf opened his heavy eyelids and muttered, 'What's up? What do you want?'

'The foreman needs you at once,' I said.

Yusuf cleared his throat, grumbled, and raised the blanket off himself; he was still in his daytime clothes!

'Will I ever rest more than two hours without work?' he said. 'So this means I can't relax?'

I said the prayer for convalescents, 'May evil never touch you, prince.'

He sat up in his bed and gave the traditional response, 'And may you never see it. By God, this isn't living, Yacoub. This isn't living.'

'But where'd you get that…box?'

'The gramophone? Do I have anything left besides that box?'

'You have records, too.'

'My wife left me, and my son too, God destroy him. He went to Italy and became a monk. And I don't know how to put away a penny, like a good upstanding man.'

'Hang in there, man.'

Without looking at me, he said, 'By God, this isn't living, this isn't living.'

I squatted near the records and began reading their names and delighting in their polished touch. There weren't more than ten, and some of them were cracked or had broken edges. Yet they looked to me like a vast fortune.

'Won't you let me visit you sometimes to hear these songs?' I asked.

'You're welcome to, every day. But beware of them. That singing there has only served to bring destruction on this house of mine.'

I laughed in amazement and said, 'Singing?'

'What do you think I did in Egypt? I fell in love with Mounira al-Turkiya, whose records you see there. A throat like silver, like gold, like the springs of paradise, and a face like roses, or carnations. But then what? She threw me out of her house without even the shirt on my back... Hand me that jar, please.'

I handed it to him. He poured water into his palm, splashed it on his face, and repeated the process two or three times while he said, 'A throat like gold, like water, clear and pure.'

He took a soiled khaki handkerchief from his pocket and wiped his face.

'Hurry up, Yusuf,' I said. 'We have a lot of work today.'

He stood up, took his pack of cigarettes from his breast pocket, and lit one, saying, 'Can't a man get a little sick sometimes? By God, this isn't living.'

We went down the stairs. 'Then will you let me play some of your records?' I asked.

'Of course, anytime. But when you come, bring me two glasses of arak, Yacoub. Okay?'

'Where am I supposed to find arak?'

'It's necessary, very necessary.'

'All right, all right.'

Our house had a small window near the ceiling through which, in the evenings, high-pitched songs would reach us from the gramophone of our neighbors, Abu Abdallah's family. Whenever I heard the singing, I would listen to it intently and delightedly, despite the fact that our neighbors' record collection wasn't extensive. If a guest visited us in the evening and sharp sounds burst forth from the skylight, we would explain, saying, 'Our neighbors have a gramophone.' The guest would move his head to express his realization of our neighbors' importance. Once I dared go up with my father to visit Abu Abdallah's family in their room. I saw the singing-box, its jaws wide open, and inside it a glistening record. In that moment, how I wished they would play it! But I was too shy to ask. The gramophone remained silent, and I left, returning to our room with a great deal of disappointment.

Later on, it seemed that the serenity of the late spring night delighted our neighbors so much so that they began playing their records one by one. Meanwhile, I lay on a mattress on the ground, reading my magazine. I was exhausted from the exertion of the day, but the article on chamber music in the eighteenth century thrilled me enough to keep me from dozing off. The strange foreign names performed within me the work of edification and enchantment, and I wasn't able to ascertain whether those sharp, shrill melodies that I heard, which sometimes imitated the cries of women, were the same kinds of melodies that the article discussed. I associated the two until my head fell upon my shoulder in a doze, in which I saw Yusuf in the clothes of a prince lowering the needle onto the record on his gramophone, whereupon his face broke out into lines and wrinkles as he sang with torment and agony. I woke up and said, 'I've got to go to Yusuf's hut right now!'

My mother objected. 'But it's almost eight,' she said. 'Have you seen any boys your age wandering the streets at such an hour?'

'I'll come back right away,' I said. 'Foreman Hanna ordered me to deliver Yusuf a letter, and I forgot. And Yusuf's hu…house is really close to ours, Mamma.'

The street, filled during the day with the ring and crack of blacksmiths' hammers, was now eerily calm. But I took heart, hurried to the wooden gate, and pushed it open. From the bottom of the stairs, I saw lines of light between the hut's planks, and yelled, 'Yusuf!'

He emerged like a ghost, gazed down at me from the raised platform, and squinting because of the height, said, 'Who is it? Yacoub?'

'Yes.'

'Come on up.'

When I went up, he said, 'Hey, where's the arak?' His mouth exuded the smell of anise.

'Where am I supposed to get arak, man?'

'Doesn't your father drink? Isn't there a bottle lying around your house you can steal two glasses from? Isn't that what friends are for, Yacoub?'

I gazed inside his hut to verify the existence of the

gramophone and records. 'I've come to hear some music,' I said.

'All right. But…all right, come on in.'

We sat on the ground and played a side of one of the records. But Yusuf was distracted, silent – not his usual self. Then he grabbed the bottle, raised it to his mouth, and took a swig. He grimaced for a moment, then said, 'Ahhhh…'

Suddenly he said, 'Listen. Will you buy it?'

'What?'

'The gramophone.'

It never occurred to me that something like that was possible. 'But how?' I asked, astonished.

'For two pounds.'

'Are you dreaming, prince?'

'It and the records for two pounds, okay? I have a plan. An important one. And money is crucial.'

'What's your plan?'

'What do you care? The gramophone and the records for two pounds. Imagine, Yacoub! Music will be at your fingertips, night and day… Imagine…'

He took me by the hand, got up, and led me down the stairs, saying, 'I have a plan, and it has to be put into action. I've saved a few pennies from this life of begging. But I need two pounds. And a bit of arak…'

As I took leave of him at the gate, I said, 'I wish I had that much money. I wish!'

At noon on Saturday, Hanna al-Mawasiri was in a state of joy that only a large sum of money could bring him. It seemed the zinc and copper ingots we'd made that week were a lucrative deal. And he didn't scrimp on a bit of baksheesh for me and Yusuf, on top of our daily wages, which he paid us every Saturday afternoon. This time he exceeded his usual generosity and said, 'We're not going to work this afternoon. What do you think about that, Yusuf? And you, Yacoub?'

'You're amazing,' Yusuf said, 'truly amazing!' His face shone with joy, and he tightened his belt so that his torn, patched pants wouldn't slip off his waist.

'Buy yourself a book today,' Hanna told me. 'Here are ten more pennies.'

'Thanks, boss!' I yelled. I went home, my hands clutching the pennies in my pocket.

At home my mother prepared a hot bath for me. I used to bathe in a large tin basin that we'd put in the kitchen. After the bath, I went out for a walk in the city streets, and every once in a while, I'd stop at the doors of cafes, where songs would be playing, just to listen. When I returned at the end of the day, I was startled by a voice coming from our room. It was Yusuf telling my father about Cairo, Tanta and Alexandria. My parents were listening, enchanted by the magic of his words. It was the first time he'd come and visited with us. What a wondrous transformation! I found him wearing new pants, a clean shirt, and a jacket without patches!

When I served the coffee, Yusuf took his cup and said, 'God bless this son of yours, Abu Yacoub. He's endowed not only with intelligence, but with excellent morals too. I'll tell him, 'Go and buy yourself something to eat,' and he'll say, 'No, I'll buy myself something to read'... I used to devour books too, when I was a child. Every book's a wonderful world where the reader can live apart from our own, full as it is of shame and disgrace. Is there anything better than reading in a world like ours, a world one's embarrassed to belong to? Wherever you look, you see nothing but declining morals and defeated virtues: Friends betray each other, sons rebel against their fathers, mothers conspire against their daughters, the well-fed devour the hungry, and the hungry want to prey on everyone. Oh yes, a book is the best companion, as the poet once said. But when I grew up, I got too busy for books. What with, you ask? With the world... The world is full of wonders, Abu Yacoub, wonders...' He sipped up the last of his coffee.

My mother said, delighted no doubt by his praise of my moral virtues, 'Why don't you come visit us sometimes, since you live nearby?'

'Why not?' he said. 'I'd be honored to.' He got up. Suddenly I saw the gramophone in a corner near the door, whose presence I hadn't noticed for my absorption in our guest's conversation. Yusuf headed towards it, picked it up by its handle, and took leave of my father at the door. Then he turned to me and said, 'Walk with me a spell.'

I went out with him, wondering whether he wanted to give me the gramophone – or lend it to me? But as soon as we reached the alley, he said, 'I didn't bring up the matter in front of your parents so they wouldn't get angry with us. I've brought you the box.'

'For me?' I cried out.

'For you to buy it.'

'But where am I supposed to get two pounds?' I asked, disappointed.

'Do you think it's easy for me to part with it? This box is the only thing I still have from my glory days. I've sold everything, but I said, by God, I won't sell this box, no matter what happens. I squandered my money, came back from Egypt, and lived like an animal in that hut. And I still didn't sell the gramophone. But I have a certain affair, an important matter, tonight. Here – I won't sell it to you. I'll pawn it to you. Give me one pound, and I'll leave it with you – along with the records, of course. Just one pound. And it'll stay yours until I give you the pound back… No, come to think of it, it's won't be necessary for you to give it back then. Just keep it until I ask for it back one day.'

'But Yusuf, I don't have a pound.'

I put my hand in my pocket to feel the silver pieces that I did have, and I imagined the extent of my elation if I got the gramophone. But seventy-three pennies were all I had.

'Well, find one, Yacoub.'

Suddenly I took out all the coins in my pocket. 'This is all I have,' I said.

He was astonished to see them in my hand, as if he hadn't expected me to remove that amount from it. He put the gramophone on the ground and said, 'All right, hand it over, and here you go.'

I emptied the coins from my hand into his and took back five pennies. He didn't object.

'And the records?'

'Come and get them.'

Elated by my lucrative deal, I hurried along with him to his hut to take the records. I was on the verge of leaving him when he stopped me, saying, 'I saw a stack of magazines in your house.'

'Yep.'

'Could you give them to me?'

'But they're old.'

'No problem. Give them to me to amuse myself with.'

I used to collect all the magazines I bought, supposing that one day I would reread them. But I didn't hesitate to return with Yusuf to give him some of them, telling myself I'd reclaim them a few days later. We entered my family's one-room apartment. My parents greeted him again, and we put the gramophone and the records to the side. Then Yusuf took the stack of magazines, in its entirety, in his arms, and I said in protest, 'Are you gonna read all of them? Just take a few.'

He winked at me, as he had in the foundry, laughed a throaty laugh, and said, his chin above the load of magazines, 'What business do I have reading at my age, Yacoub? I'll sell them by the pound and make a few pennies!' Then he added, 'And as soon as I take the gramophone back, I'll return their value to you, one by one.'

'No problem,' my father said. 'Don't worry about it. Take them, man.'

Yusuf left with the magazines piled in his arms.

Then my father asked me, 'Does Yusuf drink?'

'Yes,' I said.

He laughed and said, 'Looks like he began his night at home before visiting us this evening. Isn't it a Saturday? Seems that tonight he's in urgent need of money .'

Then we turned our attention to the gramophone and began playing and replaying records. My mother was smiling, joyful and triumphant, and said, 'All our neighbors will be amazed. Umm Abdallah will say, 'Looks like the Abu Yacoub family *also* has a gramophone.'' Quoting the proverb to ward off the evil eye, she said, 'May a stick put out the eye of the envious.'

On Monday morning, I went to the foundry, where I saw Yusuf in his usual shabby clothes. Beaming, I called out to him, 'Good morning, prince!'

But he responded with a morose grumble, 'Good morning,' and didn't look at me. When I tried to speak with him, he responded with resistance and brevity, and I realized that he didn't want to talk. So I withdrew to my work.

After a while, Foreman Hanna entered and took off his jacket, saying, 'Goddamn, man! What have you done, prince?'

He looked at the foreman with defeated eyes and said, 'They told you?'

'Of course they told me.'

'They're all bastards.'

Hanna guffawed and said, 'Dirty old man… Drink's not enough for you?'

'Are you not a human being, Hanna?' he asked with pained supplication. 'Tell me, by God, are you not a human being made of flesh and blood?'

'You found no one but Subhiya to set your sights on?'

'It's either Subhiya or no one at all…'

'How many people did you feed and water all night, and on your own tab?'

'Four, five, no, actually, it was six…'

'In order to please her?'

'Yes. But what's the use?'

Hanna guffawed again, then approached him and said, 'She didn't let you—'

'Who said that? I kissed her, by God, I kissed her!'

'Okay, I believe you, I believe you.'

A few moments later, Yusuf turned towards the foreman and said, 'Foreman Hanna. Would you like to buy a pair of pants? They're new. Only been worn once.'

'Does it come with a suit jacket too?'

'No.'

'Where's the jacket?'

'I sold it that night. The money I had wasn't enough for the evening's expenses, so I sold it to Abu Shlomo. By God, this isn't living, Hanna. Three hundred pounds I've spent in two months, on drink, laughs, women, and—'

'Enough, that's enough,' Hanna said, cutting him off. 'Get on with your work. We have new molds to make today. Yacoub! How many kilos of zinc do we still have?'

'About thirty kilos,' I said.

'Not bad,' he said. 'Let's start by making the molds.'

The Fight

Our neighbors' voices rang out as they quarreled. The insults began spewing from their mouths with such extreme violence that I was almost trembling with fear. My mother came to me. 'Go inside, son,' she said. 'Those women are shameless. Don't listen to what they're saying.'

I went inside our house, and was scared, though I didn't know why. I threw myself on the floor, trying to shut my ears to the bickerers' screams. But the screams poured over my head, gushing. The window was broken, so closing it was useless. Also, my mother refused to close the door because she needed the daylight to patch my father's socks. But after a while, I surrendered to sleep as I thought about the rugged, rocky path that led to the valley where I'd gone two or three days before to help the olive pickers. In their great generosity they gave me so many olives that I could hardly carry them all home. I dreamed that I descended to the valley again. The olive pickers were there, dancing and singing the harvest song *Ala dalouna*. One of them, a woman, pointed to me and said, 'Look at that boy, how beautifully he dances!' There I was, dancing among them until laughter overtook them all and someone picked me up and threw me to the top of the tree, loaded with black olives. The olives lay scattered on the ground, and the dancers bent down to gather them in their laps. I don't remember the dream's ending, because other dreams soon tossed me about. The sound of fighting still resounded, albeit muddled, in my ears, until I woke with a start. The forearm I'd lain my face on had fallen asleep.

The stridency of the fight had abated and become a kind of rebuke; the two parties were exhausted. Then there followed a total silence in which we could hear the chickens behind our house. As she sewed and patched, my mother began singing, in a low voice, a sad song that I listened to attentively while I lay on the floor. My soul was troubled as I felt the sadness seep within my chest and stir up obscure thoughts I couldn't quite follow. I remembered that I'd once seen my mother, a while ago, singing that same song as tears fell from her eyes, and then I too had cried, without knowing the meaning of our tears. But I didn't shed even one this time because, despite my sadness, I could still hear the voices of the fighters mingled with the songs of the olive pickers, whom I'd seen dancing in my short nap. I got up, stood in the doorway, and asked my mother the reason for the fight. 'Some people just love to bicker,' she said.

I realized somehow that the matter would be difficult for a young person like me to understand. So I stepped outside. 'You'd better not come back late!' my mother yelled after me. 'I swear, if you don't come back before sundown, I won't let you have any dinner!' Since I'd heard those words from her many times before, they didn't have much of an effect on me. I ran off to a friend's house that stood alone on a low hill overlooking small gardens of pomegranate, fig and mulberry trees. I found my friend eating bread and cheese. His father was sitting on the ground smoking a pipe, long-stemmed and yellow, and exhaling the smoke from his nose, the effect of which had yellowed that part of his moustache just below the nostrils.

I stood in awe of his visage. I regretted bursting in on them, so I retreated two steps and knocked on the door as if to apologize for failing to ask permission to enter. Then I approached with extreme respect and kissed his father's hand, for my friend was in the habit of kissing my father's hand. But the smell of pipe smoke mingled with the smell of onions that emanated from his venerable hand to my nose. I was disgusted by that gratuitous kiss, although the old man did absolve me of my abrupt entrance. 'Give your friend some bread and cheese,' he said to his son. Then he asked me, as I chewed on a delicious bite, 'How's your father doing?'

'He's well, thank God. He sends you his greetings,' I said. I thought of something better to say, but he stretched out his legs such that I understood it wouldn't be proper for me to continue talking, because I was young. He was very old.

My friend and I left, eating bread and cheese. The sun was approaching the western horizon, and it cast our shadows to a wondrous length. 'I wish we were as tall as our shadows!' my friend said.

'I wish!' I said. 'Then we'd be like the djinn, making miracles and magic.'

'Then we could get lots of money and become rich.'

'Yeah. And we'd go to the city and eat in restaurants where they sit on chairs.'

As I said that, I remembered how, a few days ago, our neighbor Abu Khalil had brought some large chairs with multi-colored patterns to his home. I also suddenly remembered his wife Umm Khalil, the fiercest fighting woman in our neighborhood, with the sharpest tongue of them all. 'I wish I could travel,' I added.

'Why?' he asked.

'Because our neighbors are always fighting with each other. I wish we could go somewhere far away and never see them again.'

My friend shot me a glance whose meaning I understood when he said, 'Wanna go to the valley?' He put all the power and temptation he could muster into his question.

'Let's go!' I said.

The Fight

We went down to the main road and from there to some little gardens, jumping over their walls until we reached the mouth of the valley. Then we started jumping from rock to rock, trying to outstrip one another, until we stopped at the entrance to a cave where rainwater had gathered. We yelled and listened as the cave returned the echo of our yells. Then we hurled rocks in the water until it splashed so much that our clothes got wet.

While we were playing, we found some snails and picked them up, laughing. Then we headed back home.

When I got back home, I found that my father had returned from the quarry where he worked. My mother was washing his feet in a metal basin and telling him the story of the fight. But as soon as my father saw me, he called me to him, took his feet out of the basin, and sat me on his lap. I noticed that his moustache was black, without any yellow in it, because he didn't smoke.

'I brought you something tasty,' my father said. 'Guess what it is?'

'An apple!' I said on the spot.

From his pocket he took out a large apple, red on one side and yellow on the other, and offered it to me. I quickly put the snails that were in my hand on the ground. I took the apple. 'When are we gonna leave this house, Daddy?' I asked.

'When God wills,' he said.

'And when *will* God will?' I asked.

He laughed and said, 'When you grow up and get a job.'

I bit into the apple. A memory of the little gardens, full of apples and grapes, floated through my mind, and I said to myself, *When I grow up and get a job, I'll buy myself a little vineyard, and I'll be able to go down to the valley at night. And there I'll sing lots of songs with my friends, and I'll serve them apples and grapes.* Then I bit into the apple once more.

When he saw me daydreaming, he said, 'When your mother serves the food, I'll tell you a great story my friend told me during lunch.'

I was delighted. I waited while my mother emptied the basin of dirty water and returned it to its place. Then she went inside the house and lit the candle. We followed her, my father and I, and sat cross-legged on the carpet, ready for dinner to arrive so that we could take pleasure in the story. My mother placed the food in front of us as the steam wafted gracefully from it, twisting and turning in the air. My father had hardly said 'Once upon a time, and on God we depend…' before a terrifying yell rent the night air, followed by a high-pitched feminine scream. My father leaped outside in one bound, and my mother hurried after him. Soon I heard our neighbors' feet rushing towards the source of the noise. Then there was a great tumult with violent, indiscernible voices, and I said to myself, *No doubt the fight's begun again.* My uncanny sense that an atrocious crime had been committed returned that odious tremor to my body.

When I left to investigate, a number of women were wailing, and many people had gathered around something lying on the ground. No one paid me any attention as I darted between the legs in the crowd. Suddenly I saw a man stretched out – and knew immediately it was Abu Murad. His head was covered in blood. Umm Murad had thrown herself upon his chest, wailing and lamenting frightfully. I retreated, slipping again in and out between people's legs, and went home, where the food still lay on the ground with steam no longer rising from it. I loathed the sight of it. I sat down on the ground, and the images got mixed up in my imagination with the clamor and screaming once again, and I saw myself running in fields filled with trees bursting with blossoms, where the daisies twinkled like stars in the green grass. But something frightening, I didn't know what, was following me, and fangs protruded from it like a dog's canines, and when it seized me, I awoke from my sleep in fright and found that I was still alone in the house. I didn't know where my parents had gone.

When I opened my eyes the next morning, I heard my father say to my mother, 'I spent the whole night in the hospital with poor Abu Murad, but he only regained consciousness for a few moments. Then he gave up the ghost.'

'God rest his soul!' my mother said.

'We thought our neighbor Abu Khalil was a righteous man,' my father said. 'Who would have believed he was capable of striking such an awful blow on Abu Murad's head with his staff?'

'God save us from that evil woman,' my mother said. 'Abu Khalil only did that because his wife provoked him. His wife can never get her fill of evil, as if the daytime fight with Umm Murad and the rest of the women hadn't been enough.'

'Who knows now how many years Abu Khalil will be in jail?' my father said.

'There's no power or strength save in God Almighty,' my mother said.

I got up then, ate some bread and olives, and had a cup of tea; that was our breakfast every day. The neighborhood was quiet, and the sound of the chickens could be heard clearly from behind our house.

Across the Wasteland

I would feel just a bit presumptuous in my criticism of Jabra Ibrahim Jabra's narrative output if I were to regard his short story collection *Arak* and his novel *Cry in a Long Night*, published previously, as only short stories, and not as poems, too. By this, I do not intend to frighten the reader or trap him into thinking that he has been deceived in his purchase – just as I do not wish to misrepresent these stories or to enter, by way of this confused and chaotic babble, into an academic study of the connections between the short story and the poem. What I mean, above all, is that these stories, which I will examine, are, in my view, not built upon event, character or dialogue so much as they are upon *symbols and suggestions*, which the author drops, with versatility and with care, here and there, just as poets do in their verses.

The stories in this book and in the novel *Cry in a Long Night* were written in different locations and milieux – Jerusalem, Baghdad, London, and Boston – and in different stages over the last ten years. Yet one finds the gulf between one story and another rather narrow, connected as they are by more than one bridge. Take, for example, the author's return, time and again, to that same world from which he drew inspiration and then went about recreating; for example, the figure of the hero, who is ever and always the same, even if he is called by different names, and even if the roles he is given differ in their value from one story to another; for example, the pure symbolism, even if the shadows differ slightly here and there.

At the forefront of those symbols is the city. Our understanding and study of Jabra's stories depend upon our consideration of the appearance of that city and its relationship with the protagonist. Jabra, as the poet of the city in modern Arabic literature, can hardly put it out of his mind, as if it were standing there before him, whenever he went to write, like a loathsome bogeyman that Jabra then attacks and tramples only to find it still standing, just as it had been. Someone other than myself could study this phenomenon on a purely sociological basis and tie the hero's relationship with the city to the author's rural boyhood and his social aspirations. But I would consider such a study secondary in importance, as it would not fully explain the phenomenon, and would not justify the author's concern, over many long years and in numerous poems and stories, with dissecting that corpse – the city – in an indirect and symbolic way. It would also be far from correct to imagine that the city the author turns his attention to is a *certain city in particular*, or that it is a city, and not a village or a town, as if the author were a new Romantic, concerned with returning to primitivity and nature. For Jabra, the city is a symbol, and not a reality. If the reader were to insist on knowing that city's name or seeing its plan, he might as well insist on knowing the names and plans for the Celestial City or the City of Destruction in Bunyan's *Pilgrim's Progress* or for the castle in Kafka's *The Castle*, or for the Wasteland in T. S. Eliot's famous poem. Everyone is free to interpret symbols as he likes, and according to the lens he uses: a Marxist lens emphasizes what a Freudian lens does not, and neither of them brings to light what a Christian or an existentialist lens would, among others. Which lens is the most correct? Do you remember the story of the elephant and the ten blind men?

The scene of events in most of these stories is the city. Yet in a few, we accompany the hero before he arrives, glimpsing what impels him to explore it. In his boyhood, the protagonist knows that he must wander, that he must abandon his village and repair to the city, where he will grow up. Although he does not know why he must do that, his ignorance does not disturb him, for he realizes that he is still young and thus that there are things he is excused from understanding. So he leaves that for the days to come.

The protagonist spends his boyhood in abject poverty. Yet he also lives in bliss and contentment. He has become accustomed to his environment; he is satisfied with it; and he has seen in it the beauty he seeks and the serenity he loves, for it is there that 'The men, women and children were singing and striking their palms together, glasses of arak before the old men, who sat cross-legged in the reticulate shadows beneath the thin branches, singing *Ala dalouna*, then stopping to hold their breath and stay their voices while the oud player sent forth a sigh of *Oooooof...*.' Even the poverty that pains him does not darken the world before his eyes. In 'Singers in the Shadows,' the protagonist goes to a feast and feeds himself on the hope of meat, but he is forbidden from tasting even one bite. Yet he cares not, and eats his dry bread as if it were a choice cut of meat. As he eats the bread, we see his feet, described to us on their way to the feast as 'dusty,' being washed in the clear, pure water.

He is then in a state of innocence. Yet that innocence will not last. 'The innocent and the beautiful have no enemy but time,' says Yeats in one of his poems, and time will slaughter that innocence and transfigure that beauty. In the story 'The Fight,' we witness a certain development that befalls the environment the protagonist inhabits. We witness his primal innocence as it begins to disappear, leaving behind the bitterness of experience. The only thing that remains of the environment is poverty, and now it is a painful, agonizing kind of poverty. The serenity and mirth it once contained have now faded; nothing remains except for the fights erupting between the neighbors, the sounds of curses and screaming, and the constant fear that they excite in the boy's soul. His world has begun to transform into two contradictory ones: the world of reality and the world of the dream; the world as it is and the world as he wishes it were. He hears curses and insults and dreams of dancing and singing; he lives in poverty and dreams of heaps of presents and gifts that he can barely carry home; he sees people come together only to clash and fight, yet he dreams that they meet to go olive-picking. The boy always awakens from his dreams to hear the fights still raging. He has begun to feel that the world he inhabits is not one he wishes to be a part of. He now strives to leave for a 'faraway place,' to go 'to the city.' This migration has become the object of his dreams, the object of his intimate conversation with his friend, and the object of conversation within his family. The boy's father places his responsibilities squarely in front of him and explains that he must move away from his environment when he grows up. When his father begins telling him a story in order to offset the noise from outside and the lethal environment surrounding him, the sound of fighting returns to interrupt the story, and the necessity of leaving becomes even clearer to the hero. Whenever he tries to escape from reality (in dreams, in stories, in planning his future), he still remains *amidst that environment*; he has not in fact escaped it yet. The neighbors' fight eventually produces a crime; death descends on the neighborhood; and even the young protagonist's dreams are stained with blood. His dreams do not return to him clear and pure to spirit him away from his environment; instead, they mix with it such that they come to resemble it, strengthening in him the longing to leave: 'I saw myself running in fields filled with trees bursting with blossoms, where the daisies twinkled like stars in the green grass. But something frightening, I didn't know what, was following me, and fangs protruded from it like a dog's canines, and when it seized me, I awoke from my sleep in fright.'

Beginning in his childhood, the protagonist Amin, from the novel *Cry in a Long Night*, is portrayed as awaiting the time when he will be able to enter the city. He has understood that he must enter it for one reason or another. Poverty did its work upon him, and he grew yet more convinced that he must explore the city. His father died and 'we had to move to the city like refugees.' Experience destroyed innocence, and sin entered the picture and began to pursue him, cracking its bloody whip, both in his lived reality and in his dreams. So he had no choice but to go to the city. The city has become, in his view, a land of milk and honey to which he came with hopes, aspirations, and visions, and which he imagined would be the refuge that would grant what had been forbidden him. So he set out, striving to take from it, to extract its riches.

But the city was not what he had hoped. Amin set out for it after the death of his father and left behind him 'the hills, valleys and vineyards' – but for what? For 'the dark quarter, with its grave-like houses, overflowing toilets, and polluted air.'

In the rest of Jabra's stories, when the hero reaches maturity, we encounter descriptions of the city, symbols of it – not as the hero first imagined it, but as he found it after living there. Now it is no longer a city, a *metropolis*, but a city of the dead, a *necropolis*; not a land of milk and honey, but a devastated, barren land. As if the city's description is a new literary image of an old myth, the myth of the Wasteland, beset by a curse, dried and withered after so much fertility, in whose people any glimmer of life has been concealed.

The city, then, as the hero finds it, is a region of death. Not actual death, but even more dreadful: spiritual death, which modern literature and thought have discussed and call death-in-life. The city's inhabitants are dead, 'dead of their hearts' hunger,' and bereft of goals and aspirations, not because they fail in what they aim or aspire to, but because *they do not know, fundamentally, what they want.* They are weary; languor has overcome them; they possess human bodies, but bodies without life, without souls. One of them calls his house 'hell,' another calls the city's alleys 'the inferno,' and a third sums up the city with a terrifying image: 'I'd like to take you by the hand, Rashid, and lead you, like Virgil led Dante, through the Hell of the Old City, and show you layer upon layer of people writhing from disease, children competing with dogs for a bone in the trash, and women crying out to God from the hunger gnawing at their insides. There you'll see one man knife another for the sake of a penny, and women sinking their fingernails into each other's faces for a few coins won by a pallid, emaciated child of theirs. Then perhaps you'd faint and fall to the ground like a rigid corpse...'

There is no creation in the city, no movement, no activity. In the city of these stories, we never hear the clamor of construction, we never see action or life, and we do not feel its heart beating – despite the fact that it is not a large, decrepit, or old city but a young one, as it seems; yet without the energy of youth or its hopes. There is no sound in the city, no fury. Its denizens may think about getting revenge on an enemy, but revenge does not pass beyond their thoughts. One of them kills his rival in a love affair, but he kills him in his daydreams, not in reality. And the city's people are incapable of making decisions. If one of them is, by chance, lucky enough to decide something, he fails to carry it out.

The stories' characters do not try to redeem time but instead contrive to kill it. The cafe is the only place that unites them, and the small cups of tea and bottles of arak are the only form of communion that links one person to another in this Wasteland – an unconstructive, unproductive, foolish communion, and from which there proceeds no elation of the spirit but instead a nausea that pervades the room. Arak is the only refuge whose shelter they seek, to numb their nerves and kill their senses. If it were in their power to numb themselves further, they would do so. If it were in their power to withdraw from life entirely, they would do so, and suicide would spread like wildfire. But suicide calls for determination and will, which they lack. Only once in these stories do we witness a character commit suicide – in 'The Deep River' – and even then it is committed under vague circumstances. On another occasion, we see a young woman resort to suicide – in 'The Two Sisters and a Flower of Thorns' – yet she takes all the precautions beforehand so as not to die. But there is no need for the city's people to commit suicide, to ask for death in return for life, for *they are already dead* – dead in this life.

The city contains only grief, disgrace, and vulgarity. It contains only 'the vileness of hunger and disease, the ugliness of houses touched by neither fresh air nor sunlight, and the lowness of life lengthened by the years, yet unacquainted for a single day with the taste of love.' The people of the city themselves see these abominations, feel their presence, and talk about them, *yet only for the sake of talking*, not out of the hope of rectifying them. They talk about them with indifference, without remorse, and without a program for reform. They talk about them because they are incapable of talking about higher matters, about greater things, about meaningful experiences. They all talk about low, base, vulgar things as if they were the woman whom Jabra, in *Cry in a Long Night*, likens to 'a gargoyle scowling from above a basin, spewing sewage from its mouth.' And when we *do* meet a character who fails to see the banality and squalor around him, but instead sits on his doorstep strumming his oud and singing – well then, that man is indeed noble, but blind as well. We may see the people of the city discussing intellectual and literary matters, but they do so in grungy, public cafes, and we sense immediately that they are merely repeating phrases they have heard, and that they return to the same issues day after day without the slightest progress. The characters in these stories are half-cultured. Occasionally, great words about important matters will emanate from their lips. But those words do not produce any effect on their lives. They are always talking about the same thing; indeed, *they are always talking*. As if their conversations were monologues, as if they themselves are gramophones replaying the same records over and over. Those long conversations and debates of theirs are also a symbol of *boredom in the city*, a symbol of slow, yawning motion, of decay, decadence, and demise. The conversations are not an end in themselves but a means of escape from their leisure and ennui – like the arak that they flee to. For them, speech is the means by which they deceive themselves such that they feel, in the words of Jean Cocteau, that they are free. They waste that freedom in limitless chatter, like the man who runs and runs, faster and faster, because he is scared. The characters in Jabra's stories, the people of the city that he paints for us, are garrulous because they are scared. They talk a lot, like the sick. They talk a lot – because they are sick.

Yet boredom, idleness, and leisure are all so ingrained in the city that its inhabitants cannot outwit them through continuous talk. Boredom is common to all, and the cafes swarm with people because they provide a temporary, superficial opportunity to do away with their ennui. As they sit in cafes most of the day and night, without stirring and without work – imagine if one of their friends rushed by for some reason or another. In that case, his friend would find it odd and ask him, 'Why the hurry? Do you have work or something?' Paralysis has stayed them all; they have all been stricken by the curse, which one of the characters in these stories affirms will afflict all the city's inhabitants. They have been stricken by what the American critic Yvor Winters calls 'the soul's slumber', which he described as 'the gravest deadly sin'. Even the most severe and profound problems of the individual do not provoke him. In the story 'Arak', Abbas reprimands his friend Mustafa because he does nothing while the woman he loves will soon be married to his rival Khalil: 'Soon he'll marry Umayma, and what will you do then? You'll sit here with me, in the cafe, and count the people coming and going.' The greatest disaster in the city is that its people are *incapable of action* – not that they do what they should not. In an article by Eliot on Baudelaire, he writes that 'So far as we are human, what we do must be either evil or good; so far as we do evil or good, we are human.' Eliot adds, 'And it is better, in a paradoxical way, to do evil than to do nothing.' For in that instance, at least we have affirmed our existence. The people of the dead city cannot even do evil; they do nothing, and their very existence is an object of doubt.

In the city, proper human relations do not obtain between one individual and another. There is no true companionship, contact, or unity. Social bonds are nonexistent, solitude reigns, and every man is an island, detached from others and devoid of any feeling of responsibility towards society and other people. And no wonder, for the modern city is dead. The modern city is hell. As the English poet Abraham Cowley wrote four centuries ago, 'I call this city hell and chaos, where every man is concerned with himself and no one is concerned with others.'

Such spiritual estrangement is one of the most prominent aspects of the Wasteland. Jabra depicts that estrangement powerfully for us through simple events that do not mean much in themselves – and that do not add or subtract much from the context of the story – yet that serve as symbols, thus appearing important. The characters' relationships with each other are forever trivial: they meet over a glass of arak or a cup of coffee and talk nonsense or debate each other about important issues, but in a manner that renders those issues trivial, simple, ordinary. The characters are lost. Even the cat in *Cry in a Long Night* is 'confused.' The people of the city are anonymous and unknown. They have no names, no being, no personality, no bonds between them. When they do congregate outside a cafe, they do not do so in a social circle, club or place of worship but in the cinema, where darkness destroys any bonds that could spring up between them, and from which they are ejected two hours later, only to end up as they had been before. The people of the city are mere forms with no being: in *Cry in a Long Night*, the protagonist walks through the city's Great Square, 'the heart of the city,' and all he sees are 'black shapes of men standing in doorways, expelled by the stream of humanity. They leaned on walls with cigarettes dangling from their mouths, their hands planted deep in their pockets.' As he continues walking, alone, unable to meet anyone to talk with, heart-to-heart, as a human, someone shoots out of the shadows and addresses him – but that person is a madame, a procuress, and the conversation between them is as follows: 'Do you want a nice young lady tonight?' Another person shoots out of the darkness and extends his hand in greeting – but the man realizes a moment later that he has greeted Amin by mistake; he does not recognize him. Human contact is temporary and trivial, the result of error. The hero is alone, everyone is alone, there are no proper relationships, and there is no sure knowledge. The people live in darkness, so they cannot discern. And when they do see others, they see them in such a way that they do not recognize them, as in the description of the house the protagonist inhabits in the city:

'We all slept on the floor, and instead of electricity, our room had an awful-smelling kerosene lamp. We didn't have any windows overlooking trees or flowers, but instead chinks in the walls located just above ground level so that we could see only the legs of the passersby; we came to recognize people by their legs' (from the story 'Books and Two Handfuls of Dirt'). In these stories, we seldom encounter the characters within their homes, with their lovers, or with their friends. They are either always alone or with company yet lonely there, too; they achieve loneliness by all the different, imperfect means.

In the individual's estrangement from others, all of society becomes sick. The sick individual passes his sickness to society, and the sick society destroys the individual and infects him in turn. The spiritual emptiness of the city's inhabitants causes societal paralysis. The stench of their corpses tinges the city with corruption, and societal corruption destroys them and increases their spiritual emptiness. This is a vicious circle from which there is no escape in the dead city.

There is no love in the city, for death has taken its place. It is not that love has mingled with death, as it does in life and in literature, and especially in Romantic literature; it is rather that *death has banished love* and ascended its throne, as in the protagonist's dream in *Cry in a Long Night*. Amin dreams about Sumaya, his wife, who is, in the dream, a symbol of love sailing the lovers' boat. Yet a deathly specter attacks the boat and drowns the lovers. The characters of the city, unable to truly live, are also unable to love. It has gotten to the point where 'Love feeds death, and sex is a symbol of death,' instead of love and sex both being a symbol of the return to the womb, the return to *what was before the city*, to what is beyond it.

Love in the city is feeble, founded on repression and deprivation, both of which affect the city's men as much as its women, rob them of the splendor of life, restrain them from reproduction, and fortify in them the seeds of decay and dissolution. In the rest of Jabra's stories, we glimpse men yearning for women and women yearning for men, without either being able to effect their hopes or possess their beloved. In love, as in the other spheres of life, the people of the city are incapable of moving from cogitation to execution, from thinking to doing. It is a rigid, unmoving love, an isolated, isolating love for the lovers involved, a love that Jabra delicately and humorously refers to as 'picking the nose.' A temporary love, a love born of a spontaneous outburst that leads only to nausea. The call of love in the city is the call of pimps, and the beloved, in the city, is a woman of the night. Indeed, prostitutes in these stories are principal characters, even if they do not always appear onstage. In the city, love is emasculated. The lover suffices with talking about love and writing poems about it. In some of the stories, we read about a burning, passionate love; we read of Mustafa recalling his love for Umayma, describing it as a love located in 'her blood, by the undulations of her flesh and the folds of her brain. By her intestines, her liver and her gall bladder.' We imagine him a successful lover who has possessed his beloved and reconciled the spirituality of love with its corporeality. But we soon discover that Mustafa has instead merely written poetry about her and has only won from her 'a stolen kiss a year ago, or more.' Such degraded love reaches its climax in the character Hussein in 'Voices of the Night,' who visits a brothel regularly, goes to his favorite girl there with a poem in his hand, and returns without having touched her. To return to Mustafa from 'Arak,' his 'imagination wraps itself around Umayma's legs, but [he writes] about her eyes. [He wishes he] could pull her by the hair to the banks of the Tigris and wallow with her naked in the mud. Instead [he writes] about a passion clean and pure.'

Jabra's dead city contains no successful love, no perfect love. The bulk of the characters in these stories are single men and women enervated by sexual repression, or people who have found only brothels as an outlet for their burning lusts. Yet the married characters in these stories have also failed to attain a successful, more perfect kind of love. The character Yusuf in 'The Gramophone,' who sells the last of his earthly goods for a kiss (which he may not even have gotten) from a *cheap woman*, is no less a failure in love than the character Rashid in *Cry in a Long Night*. When Rashid gets together with his miserable, repressed, bachelor friends, he turns their attention to grand subjects like Life and Woman; he attributes their failure to their incapacity to marry, to love successfully, or to have a relationship with a woman.

Rashid is blind to the fact that his own love is unsuccessful and that his marriage has not exactly carried him to a long-awaited heaven. Perhaps one of the most prominent signs of love's defeat in the city is that the one person who defends Woman and Love is Rashid, married to a woman who not only does not love him but also cheats on him regularly. Rashid listens to his friends, regards their love as a mere selfish, sexual act, and goes about stroking his wife's body with foolish confidence in full view of his friends. But Rashid's caresses are also a kind of selfish, sexual act because they are not reciprocated. At one point, he yells in their faces with laughable haughtiness: 'You're entitled to wallowing in manure if you so desire. As for me, I have my wife.' We readers can only smile with sorrow and respond, 'And that wife of yours, isn't she so much manure?'

Love in the city, in addition to the foregoing, is a *diminished* love, for the city's men have lost their sexual potency. It is as if that curse which, so we read, must strike the city is the same curse that destroyed the sexual potency of the king in the Wasteland myth and, furthermore, the power of all his people. The city's men are 'stricken by the curse – the curse is so widespread in them that most of the city's women have become either lesbians or fallen women, because their husbands are incapable of pleasing them.' Love in the city is also diminished because it is sterile. In all these stories, we see with clarity the city's sterility and the absence of natural relationships. We read about marriages, but none that produce any children; the only time we read about a pregnant woman of the city is in 'Two Sisters and a Prickly Pear.' Yet the woman's pregnancy was not only a mendacious claim – add to that how when she claimed she was pregnant, she also claimed that she had miscarried: No fruits are borne in the dead city. In these stories, we read of a disdain for the feminine characteristics that symbolize health, strength, and the ability to bear children. We witness the interest of the city's men, during their conversations about women's bodies and the pleasure they give, turned repeatedly to their hind quarters.

In the city, we find a unique kind of company and companionship – the companionship of people in whom love has been killed off, people who refuse to move or budge. And the two phenomena are absolutely related. Just as we'll find those same characters spending their energy scolding those few characters who *have* thought about love (I won't write '*who have loved*') and destroying their love before it can even be graced with success.

In this collection's title story, 'Arak,' we read about Abbas, an accountant, 'whose fingertips had been worn down from counting dinars, yet who was unable to put any of those coins into his own pocket.' This image contains a symbolic description of the men of the city and their relationships with love and women. They talk about them all day long, they toss and turn in their beds all night for their sake, yet they are not fortunate enough to become correctly and truly acquainted with them, to enjoy them, or to reach a meaningful stage in their relationships with them.

Thus is love in the city. It resembles the statue of Aphrodite, the goddess of love herself, that stands in Roxane's courtyard in *Cry in a Long Night*. This is the statue which Amin gazes on, and in which he glimpses the goddess of love; to Amin, Aphrodite appears as a 'dry, twisting bough.' So the svelte, curvy, beautiful goddess of love appears in the dead city as a 'dry, twisting bough.'

Thus is love in the city because the curse has struck it. Death has sunk its claws into the city, and into love. Yet love is thus in the city because its people are almost wholly limited to men. Women, whom the men's conversation always revolves around, are scarcely apparent in the stories. Instead, we read *about* them and feel their presence and feel almost vengeful towards them *without hearing their voices or seeing them*, save on rare occasions. The men only speak about them in order to attack them; men's tongues only mention women so that their tongues' vitriol can cover them in their entirety. *Woman*, for the Men of the Wasteland, contains not just a body, with the potential for desire and the satisfaction of that desire, but also a mind 'not worth two cents.' *Woman* is selfish and opportunistic, concerned only with quenching an unbearable, instinctual thirst; *Woman* is sadistic, cursed, lethal; Woman is ever a locus of doubt, the source of evil and disaster. In Adnan's poem, from the story 'Voices of the Night,' there is perhaps the best summary of the *idea of*

Woman in the Dead City: 'Women extol you as a symbol of their cravings only to crucify you one day on a date palm, your mouth hanging open in the midday dust. They pour wine over your feet, then they eat your eyes, and mourn your lips, because no one is left to kiss them; then they dance around your limbs as they dismember you, piece by piece; they pour out wine over you again, then empty their bladders, so that the thorns grow, paltry and malnourished, around your remains.' *Woman* is forever an object of mockery for the city's men. Even the one thing about her that pleases them – her body – does not escape their stinging sarcasm; indeed, they pour forth their scorn and perverted jests about one of the most beautiful parts of her body, her behind. If this is the view of half the city's people towards its other half, then how can the city be safe from the curse? Indeed, the blame does not fall upon one half only, and not the other, for Woman too is dead. And in a city such as Jabra describes, it is difficult for us to blame man for his distorted view of women, for the women do not deserve much regard themselves.

In the mind of a man of Jabra's city, *Woman* is either one of two things: a woman he communes with in order to relieve purely physiological needs through that communion; and a woman he yearns to commune with but with whom, in the context of this Dead City, such communion is not feasible. So here Woman is one of two things: either unchaste or ethereal, neither of which the City of Life recognizes as a woman, through whom creation, reproduction, and salvation are hoped for. Because one of those two Woman-figures is ethereal, she remains unknown for these stories' characters, such that even if they meet her and imagine they know her, such knowledge will be only delusional and thin. Any woman who is not a prostitute is an eternal enigma for them. We see this most clearly in the short story 'Where Dreams Meet' and in *Cry in a Long Night*, where we witness Amin's ignorance of Sumaya and the catastrophes that his ignorance causes. Amin gets to know a woman who is not a prostitute, so he imagines her as ethereal and converses with her as if she were ethereal, flirts with her as if before him were not a human woman but *a supernatural being*, well above his comprehension. And in vain she tries to drag him back to reality, to convince him of the necessity of integration and union. Amin sees Sumaya's legs at the beginning of his relationship with her, and wonders aloud,

'What sculptor fashioned those calves?' I asked.

She laughed and said, 'Your imagination!'

'You look like a Greek statue,' I said. 'Maybe you're not made of marble but of flower petals.'

'No,' she said, 'I'm made of flesh and blood.'

When Amin meets Sumaya for the first time, in the midst of a thunderstorm in an uninhabited place, he asks her, 'Is the damsel in distress?' as if he were a medieval knight on a quest to save the ladies of the court. She replies with gentle mockery, with realism, with understanding: 'Yes, and I'm soaked through, too!' In the story 'Where Dreams Meet,' Anwar says to Rebab, 'You are the earth, rich with treasures; you are the sea on a moonlit night; you are the forest of the poets…You are fire in days of cold and food in days of hunger.' Rebab raises her hand to stop him and says, comically, 'Yes, Anwar, I'm all those things put together. But I'm also a weak creature – I'm afraid of catching cold when exposed to the wind; on some nights I get headaches and can't sleep; I hate certain people and would like to see them hanged in order to be rid of them.' The hero of the novel, Amin, throughout all the stages of his relationship with Sumaya – falling in love, their marriage, after she leaves him – never stops regarding her as an unsolvable enigma. He does not know why she behaves towards him as she does; he does not know why she left him when she did or why she returned when she did. She is an eternal enigma that he has never understood and *will* never understand – at least until salvation comes.

Therefore, because Woman is a prostitute, perfect love will not exist in the city; because She is unknown, true love will not exist in it either. Man regards her as either this or that, so if she is a prostitute, then she is not a person, and if she is unknown, the hero drowns her in his deification of her until he discovers that she is not qualified for deification and she returns, in his eyes, to the ranks of the prostitutes. Because he regards her thus, he does not actually know her as a woman, with the freedom to live in the city and transform it from death to life. Thus is he forever incapable of integrating those two ideas of woman into one, of regarding a woman as a person, as a creature with both a bodily and a spiritual side. Jabra's hero cannot escape from binary opposites to arrive at what Jamil in 'Books and Two Handfuls of Dirt' calls 'the period of twilight' in which 'we waver between opposites, and glimpse gardens of paradise in one moment and the abysses of hell in another, in which we could almost touch virtue with one hand and impurity with the other...The lucky few among us live in continuous periods of twilight.' It is paradoxical, then, that the character harmed by this fragmentation and division, the character who called for the necessity of integration, is Rebab. Rebab, as the reader will see, is not a realistic character but a product of the imagination; she is not a resident of the city.

This ignorance of women, this renunciation of even trying to probe the mystery, leads not only to failure in human and amorous relationships within the city, but also to the greatest calamity in the mythological context of the Wasteland. The myth emphasizes that the hero must learn the *mystery of things* if he wishes to restore to the Wasteland its fertility, its reproductive capacity, its creation. The hero must visit the Chapel Perilous and inquire about the nature of things, and only then will the curse upon the land be lifted. But the hero in Jabra's stories is incapable of that as long as he is in the city. He is not able to learn the secret. Thus the city remains dead, and he remains emasculated within it. He can almost hear the following phrases ringing in his ears, as they ring in the ears of the knight in the story of *Peredur* when he fails to inquire about the secrets and does not ask about what he sees in the Castle of Wonders: 'Hadst thou done so [i.e. asked,] the King would have been restored to health, and his dominions to peace, whereas from henceforth he will have to endure battles and conflicts, and his knights will perish, and wives will be widowed, and maidens will be left portionless, and all this because of thee.'

This, then, is the city to which the hero in Jabra's stories travels, the city he imagined would be a city of salvation and redemption but finds to be a city of destruction. What does he do?

The outcome is the same: as long as he is in the city, he has no hope of salvation. In the Wasteland myths, it is on the efforts of the knight that the king and his kingdom pin their hopes for recovery and health. But the hero of these stories is not a knight, and he does not do what the knight is supposed to do. He does not inquire about the meaning of symbols at the Chapel Perilous; he does not try to comprehend the nature of things in the city; he avoids the society around him and mocks women instead of getting to know them as people; he only gets to know the city's people by visiting cafes, as if he were a lone selfish man who does not seek to bring resurrection to the dead city – but instead as if his concern were *to be resurrected himself* and to escape the destruction surrounding him. He does not go to the city in order to save it, but instead, as the reader will remember, either because he is compelled to or because he seeks to win glory there, to gain comfort, ease and wealth. The hero does not come to give to the city but to take from it. Thus throughout his stay there, he does not escape the germs that emanate from it; he is exposed to them, as are the city's people themselves. In the rest of the stories, we see the hero in an unstable situation. For example, in 'Voices of the Night,' he is one of the characters and yet not one of them; he spends time with them, listens to them, speaks a little. But he regards their conversations and problems as trivial. He senses their shortcomings. He is with them most, but not all, of the time, dividing his interest and concern between their concerns and those of others. He is thus forced to leave them to travel to a different social class – to a different milieu, to horizons they are unfamiliar with. But these horizons, as we discover after a little while, are not actually wider; their class is actually no higher than that of his original friends. Indeed, he cannot leave his friends for long, so he returns to the cafe. When he does not find them there, he looks for them in a bar only to find them with their all-powerful companion, Nausea. He has become one of them to a great degree; he has become exposed to the destruction of their collective sickness. He falls ill. He has begun to regard people as sick, and the city as sick, not because the king in it is sick, but because *he* is. The doctor he could have been is sick. He has become like the people of the city. He has become like them in the judgment of the dead. He is not astonished, during his long wandering in the city's alleyways, when one of his fellow citizens meets him and addresses him, only to correct himself immediately and say, 'But I see that you are dead.'

But he is still the hero, and he still has a message. He senses that he must rise up and strive for salvation. But here, too, his understanding of salvation differs from that of the mythical knight, for our hero's striving is towards the *salvation of himself* – not the salvation of society, and not even the salvation of those few who join hands with him, such as Roxane Yasser, to whom Amin says with resolve, 'You have to search for your new life alone.' The city's salvation does not concern him. Neither does the restoration of virility to the king, nor the fertility of the land, nor the lives of people, animals and plants. All that concerns him is that *he* rise up, that *he* exit the city, that *he* find the glory, contentment, and triumph that he could not find there. His goal, then, is not to restore life to the Wasteland but to traverse it and to find triumph beyond it.

The hero now crosses the Wasteland with consciousness and awareness, and succeeds. Indeed, he does not cross it with the ignorance and compulsion with which he entered it, which caused him to fail during his tenure there. Leaving the city must be authentic and conscious. The landmarks must be clear to the hero for triumph to be possible – not like with Yusuf in 'The Gramophone,' who left his world, the city, for another. Yusuf did so by compulsion and not by choice, so throughout his life in his new world, he continues to grieve for the past he left behind and strives to return to it. Yusuf is like Lot's wife, transformed into a pillar of salt, or Eurydice, who disappeared from her husband forever.

When we recall the similarities between the author and his hero, the road by which the hero leaves the city and crosses the Wasteland becomes apparent. Jabra, in the two books before us, is doing what many writers do when they draw 'A Portrait of the Artist as a…' Jabra here is drawing 'A Portrait of the Artist as a Wasteland-Crosser.' That crosser, that hero, is an artist – and thus the path of exit and triumph can only be through art. The hero has been aware of this ever since childhood. When he lived in straitened, overburdened circumstances, he turned to books as a way out of his environment, a way to break his chains, to forget his reality. And some of the dead city's residents – towards whom the hero feels a kind of sympathy he does not feel towards other fellow citizens – realize that. One example is the character Afif in 'Closed Windows,' who finds, in singing, a kind of victory over his agonizing reality. Another is Anwar in 'Where Dreams Meet,' who leaves the city to write a book and thereby regains his trust in people. For the hero of Jabra's stories, art – and, more precisely, literature – compensates for the lack of intimacy and contact between the people of the dead city; literature is 'the point at which the contradictions canceled each other out, and the manner in which the colors, in shades of both light and dark, could be arranged harmoniously.' Literature is the refuge to which Amin flees when he fails in his amorous relationship with his wife Sumaya, who abandoned him; he thereby shifts from sterility to fertility, from the Wasteland to whatever is beyond it.

Yet the hero is an artist and not a mercenary writer, not a pen-for-hire. Thus art alone is entrusted with clearing the way forward – not writing in whatever form it may take. Accordingly, professional journalism, towards which some of the city's people are inclined, serves no purpose, and neither does writing poems and articles on political, social and moral issues, towards which others of the city's people are inclined. Also without benefit is what the hero himself takes refuge in for a time: When Amin writes, on demand, a tome on the history of Roxane's and Inayat's family, the Yassers; when he writes for hire, not for art's sake, for others and not for himself; when he aims to serve the city and society, and becomes committed, engagé, and, as if through his engagement, places a chastity belt on the sensitive members of his art instead of breaking the many chastity belts that already restrict them, instead of helping them achieve pleasure, creation, and benefit. Such engaged literature is entrusted with making the writer a productive member of society, a good citizen. But here is the problem: the hero, through this genre of committed literature, becomes a good citizen in the dead city. The tragedy is that the hero, when he flees to engaged literature, is suddenly oblivious that such lifeless literature cannot give life; neither he nor the city is animated or invigorated by it. The tragedy is that the hero wants to create and produce but wants to remain a citizen too – and the two are contradictory: for the good citizen in the dead city is dead, and one hopes in vain for creativity and productivity to spring from the deceased. As long as the hero strives for salvation, and for self-salvation above all, he must first withdraw from the city. As long as he is an artist, he must withdraw from the city through his art, and not prostitute it to social issues. If he must choose to be either a dead citizen or a creative artist, he must choose art and creation.

That is to say, the hero must reject the city. He must reject it after having experienced it, lived in it, possessed it. He must kick it away when it turns towards him; he must repel it when it throws itself upon him.

Such a triumphant refusal is what we see at the end of 'Arak.' Throughout the story, Abbas controls the situation; he is the story's obscene, poisonous tongue, the destroyer-figure who holds so much sway over Mustafa that the latter becomes like Abbas, seeing depravity in innocence and imagining that his faraway beloved is a prostitute. Abbas is the dead city, and the hero, Mustafa, through his friendship with Abbas and the close attention he pays him, has become – or almost become – like Abbas. This is all despite Mustafa's idealism, and despite that he is in love and writes poetry. But the story does not end like this. Its ending is triumphant, for Abbas takes Mustafa's books, which never leave his side, and throws them on the ground. Mustafa rises up and – here is the climax – strikes Abbas. After the fight, Mustafa returns, not to make peace with Abbas, who yearns to do so, and not to pay for the arak, but to retrieve his books, to rescue his art and his idealism from the destroyed city: 'Mustafa bent over the three books scattered on the ground, which the men milling about had trampled on during the fight, and picked them up one by one.' This triumphant rejection is also what we see in the story 'The Man Who Loved Music,' in which 'the Man' spends his life seeking wealth until he amasses more of it than anyone else in the City of Greed. Then he flees the city for the hills and tears his banknotes apart. This triumphant rejection is what we see in the novel, *Cry in a Long Night*, when the hero, Amin, rises up and is resurrected from his languor and indolence, which the city infected him with; with detachment he comes to understand his blind, shameful love. Amin was lost, perplexed, torn in his thoughts and feelings, desiring a touch, a mere touch, from Sumaya. But at the novel's climax, when she comes to him, *she* comes to *him* instead of his going to her; she comes to him in her entirety, with her whole body, with her whole soul. And he expels her, refuses to touch her, refuses to keep her in his room, and throws her out. This triumphant rejection is also what we see in 'Closed Windows,' when the hero's runaway beloved returns and displays herself before him with lust, vehemence, and persistence. He looks into her eyes and sees in them not love but lust. And because she is all the city can offer the lover, he leaves her, paying no attention to her entreaties and self-debasement before him. He leaves the house 'without looking back. It occurred to [him] that the heavens were laughing and that the city, in its clamor and uproar, was dancing and singing.' And so for the first time, the dead city dances for him, and sings. This is a triumphant, affirmative rejection – not Yusuf's kind of rejection in 'The Gramophone,' which occurs for the hero after he possesses the city, and not after he fails in it. It occurs when he realizes, like the character Europa in the tragic play *Cadmus* by Said Akl, that 'to disdain life,' if this is indeed life, 'is sweeter than life itself.'

That triumph comes to the hero at the end of his journey, when he rejects the city and leaves it behind. And along with that triumph comes resurrection, which Jabra expresses in his novel through an explosion. In the Wasteland myths, water and rain are fundamental symbols, and they must appear on the scene before the knight succeeds in his quest and carries fertility to the barren land. Water and rain appear a number of times in these stories, always heralding important events. But they never lead to a triumphant conclusion and the salvation of the city, as they do in the Wasteland myths. Water in itself will not suffice to resurrect Jabra's dead city. There is something more effective than water, and the hero must wait for it so that resurrection will be possible for him. In the Christian Gospels, beyond baptism by water lies baptism by fire – and the hero must await the fire.

The fire comes in the form of an explosion at the end of the novel. Sumaya comes to Amin, collapsing upon him, exhausted. The city opens its doors to him and grants him its golden key. Rain has started pouring. And Amin does not respond well to Sumaya's advances. But she does not back down, and repeats the attempt, confident he will relent. He almost does relent, for the baptism is still only one of water. When the great baptism does come – the baptism of fire – the sound of a powerful explosion rends the air, and Amin's anticipated resurrection appears before his eyes. After the 'long night' he has experienced, actually and symbolically, throughout the narrative, dawn has broken: 'I looked out the window, and suddenly the day had dawned, gray and clear; I hadn't even noticed.' Amin hears an explosion again and realizes clearly and distinctly that the 'night' has passed. Barrenness and sterility have ceased, and death has been defeated: 'I realized that what I saw was a purifying fire that broke out over there to finish off contagious germs – it broke out to save me, to purify my flesh and blood. I stood fixed in the window, bewitched by what I saw. I would have liked to explode in continuous laughter like the thunder of successive explosions.'

Then, and only then, is Amin able to rejoice and to scream in Sumaya's face (and the city's): 'Don't you see the fire? It's going to burn you too!' Then, and only then, does Amin recognize that he has been living in a grave, not a city. He rebels against death and escapes it, and he says to Sumaya: '[L]ook at yourself: yellow like death, withered like death. And starting today, I want nothing to do with death!' Then, and only then, does Amin escape the dead city. He crosses the Wasteland.

This salvation-through-refusal – is it negative? Is it defeatist? Anyone who has had to stand before one's past in its entirety, who has clung to that past until he has become a part of it, only to fix it with a new, penetrating gaze, who has rebelled against it as if he were tearing apart not only the past but also himself, piece by piece; anyone who has had to refute – in his heart, in his thoughts, in his very soul – a love that lived and thrived within him yet remained to him a stranger, unable to settle down; anyone who has had to let out the deepest, bloodiest scream, '*non serviam*: I will not serve,' repeating along with James Joyce's hero in *A Portrait of the Artist as a Young Man* that 'I will not serve that in which I no longer believe whether it call itself my home, my fatherland or my church'; anyone who has done all that will know that this salvation-through-refusal contains a kind of affirmation, will, and strength, and that it contains a penetration into the self seldom found in salvation-through-acceptance.

That striving for self-salvation before the salvation of society – is it not individualistic and antisocial? It may appear so until we recall that Jabra's hero is an artist and not a knight, and that his quest is not that of the knights of the Middle Ages, from which the Wasteland myths emerged; it may appear so until we recall that the hero-knight in Eliot's poem 'The Waste Land,' when he senses towards the end of the poem that reviving the land is too difficult for him, asks, 'Shall I at least set my lands in order?' and that Noah, when he left behind the land of destruction, built one ark and not an entire fleet, and did not turn to his fellow humans to rescue them. Noah realized, through divine revelation, that his fellow humans were already drowned, even before the flood. Even if they had been transported to a high mountain whose peak the waters had not reached, Noah could not have saved them. Noah realized that his humanitarian mission, his societal mission, was to leave the drowned earth for a lofty mountain, and from there to build a new society.

That is exactly what Jabra's hero does. He is an artist who strives to 'set his lands in order' and board the Ark alone, taking along his art as his only companion in order to create with it a better city and a more fertile land.

In this collection, 'The Man Who Loved Music' differs completely from the other stories; Jabra himself describes it as a 'strange story.' It is in fact an allegory in which Jabra summarizes my contention in the foregoing paragraphs about the hero's rejection of the city after having possessed it, about his distancing himself from the city, about his salvation alone from death in the city and the refuge he can find only through art. The hero of this story goes from rags to riches and achieves a high social standing. But he abandons the city unexpectedly and heads for the hills, the rocks, and the open country. While in the crowded city he lived in a 'humble home,' we read that, while on the desolate rocky hill, 'the house he built there was not a mere hut but more like a palace.' He lives by himself, listens to records, and tears up heaps of banknotes, brushing from his shoes the dirt that had collected on them ever since he left the city. He takes refuge in art, and then dies – for he has concluded his message.

This story says what the others do, but it goes further. The hero of this story does not shut the windows on himself as he listens to music. He does not bury his art but instead cranks the volume up as high as it will go and has it fill the air. That is what the Biblical Noah does – he leaves the city behind but carries with him a seed, a kernel, with which he later attacks, or overcomes, the city in order to transform it for the better. The hero in this story attacks the city with musical melodies. He attacks it not in order to take from it or to rob it, but to give to it, to resurrect it anew.

That art, to which the hero flees when he rejects the dead city and abandons it, is the very instrument for reviving the city. The way of art – which the hero treads in order to cross the Wasteland, and which is the destination of his pilgrimage – will itself be the water, the seeds, the germination that will fertilize the Wasteland, restore the greenery to its fields and the virility to its king and its youth, and wipe away from its virgins the sterility in their dreams and their bodies.

Tawfiq Sayigh
1956